PARANORMAL COZY MYSTERY

Fries & Alibis

TRIXIE SILVERTALE

Sittin' On A Goldmine
Productions L.L.C.

Sittin' On A Goldmine Productions, L.L.C.

pr@sittinonagoldmine.co

www.sittinonagoldmine.co

ISBN: 978-1-7340221-0-0

Cover Design © Sittin' On A Goldmine Productions, L.L.C.

Trixie Silvertale
Fries and Alibis: Paranormal Cozy Mystery : a novel / by Trixie Silvertale — 1st ed.

[1. Paranormal Cozy Mystery — Fiction. 2. Cozy Mystery — Fiction. 3. Amateur Sleuths — Fiction. 4. Female Sleuth — Fiction. 5. Wit and Humor — Fiction.] 1. Title.

CHAPTER 1

I WAKE UP with a pounding headache and a dry, sticky tongue. Rolling over, I'm confronted with an unpleasant odor. Oof! My sheets are way past due for a wash.

Flashes of last night's bachelorette party peek through the curtain of fog draped over my brain. A red and pink streamer tickles my forehead with fresh whispers of regret. I yank it from my hair and roll onto my feet.

The room swirls and I cradle my head as more images bubble to the surface. Did I dance on the bar at the Flicka Shack?

No. I think that was Elisa.

But I'm certain that I, the one and only Mitzy Moon, grabbed the mic from Fat Carol and screeched out an endless rendition of "My Heart Will Go On."

I wish I could say this sequence of events is a rare occurrence. No such luck. Over the years of struggling to survive in foster care I built a wall around my emotions. Now I prefer to drown them —or eat them. I exhale stale air and urge my grey matter to make a plan.

Today my To Do list will be short:

1. Take aspirin and drink two gallons of water.
2. Do as little as possible at work.
3. Apologize to Fat Carol.

Don't look at me like that—she calls herself Fat Carol. She's not even fat; she thinks it's ironic. Don't get me started.

4. Wish that I could afford to call in sick, collapse onto my sofa, and binge-watch . . . anything.

As the hydration seeps into my cells, a few more choice moments float up from the murky depths. I should probably head over to the free clinic and get a Z-pak to ward off whatever slimy creatures crawled out of Shady Ben's mouth and onto my tongue while I was licking his tonsils!

By the way, welcome to my life.

This is it: Parties. Booze. Regrets. There's a

whole sad little orphan backstory—but I'm getting ahead of myself.

I could also thrill you with tales of my amazing career at the coffee shop *du jour*, but I don't think you can handle that much excitement in one day.

Yes, I need to get a life—or at least start crowd-funding for one.

KNOCK. KNOCK. KNOCK.

Insistent, but not threatening. It's probably Jennifer stopping by on her morning run to fill me in on the dirty details of my nocturnal escapades.

Lucky for me I'm still wearing my skinny jeans and *Supernatural* T-shirt from last night. No need to wrap up in a nasty sheet.

Not that Jenn stays sober; she just has a relentless Insta. Hooray. Because there's nothing quite as wonderful as a public, online portal cataloging the breadth of my poor judgment.

Stepping over more than one insect carcass, I make my way toward the pounding assault on my aching head.

Before the door opens completely I hit her with a zinger. "So, what manner of atrocity did I commit, Jenn?"

As the wizened old man hunched in my hallway pulls into focus, my jaw falls slack like a broken ventriloquist dummy. "I was expecting someone else," I stammer.

"That makes two of us," he snipes. His bulbous nose twitches and he harrumphs into his thick grey mustache with what I assume is disdain.

Ouch.

He balances an ancient leather briefcase against the wall and rummages through the contents. His gnarled hand grasps a bulging manila envelope. He sticks the corner between his teeth—the color of the pouch blending unfortunately with the shade of his chompers. He closes the briefcase with two sharp clicks and clears his throat. Three times. His saggy cheeks flap unceremoniously.

"I'm looking for Mizithra Achelois Moon." A gust of pipe smoke and denture cream wafts toward me on the tail of his inquest.

I stare in surprise, flavored with a pinch of gut-churning horror. The last time someone came to the door and slaughtered the pronunciation of my full, legal name they followed up by informing my babysitter that a commuter train had killed my mother.

The old man shifts his pear-shape back on his heels and strains to see the number dangling from one screw on the door next to my slowly nodding head.

"Do I have the wrong apartment?" He huffs and wags his balding head.

"I'm Mitzy." I can't bring myself to say the

whole name. My late mother was the only one who called me Mizithra. It happens to be the name of a Greek cheese, and also the thing that brought her and my since-vanished father together twenty-two years ago.

Theirs had been a classic "meet cute." She was shopping at some over-priced hipster grocery store and my rumored-to-be irresistible father had reached for the same ball of mizithra cheese that my mom had grabbed. Their hands touched. Cut to her apartment. Their naughty places touched. He never called. She kept the baby.

Maybe she named me after the cheese in some strange hope that he would return and they would share a laugh. That never happened. And now she's gone too. So, it's Mitzy. Just Mitzy, okay?

Oh, crap. The old shriveled guy has been talking the whole time I took a trip down memory lane. I missed literally everything he just said. Nod and smile, my mother always said.

So I do.

He hands me the large envelope, says, "I'm sorry for your loss," and shuffles away.

Since I've lost pretty much everything, I shrug and tear open the envelope as I kick the door shut with my UN-pedicured heel.

Cash.

A key.

Documents.

Did I mention the cash?

Pushing aside yesterday's empty takeout container, I upend the envelope onto my dining-room TV tray and stare.

I don't deal with much cash in my world, but I'd have to say this particular pile of hundreds looks like a crap ton of money. I could count it, but I don't want to ruin the illusion of wealth by discovering an actual dollar amount.

I touch the crisp bills. They feel real. I'll have to sneak one to work and make a mark on it with that magic authentication pen, just to make sure it's a real "Benjamin."

Yuck. Visions of Shady Ben's hands on my body slither into my consciousness.

I need a shower.

Touching the bills one more time, I gasp and race to throw my deadbolt and chain the front door. Now that I'm rich some low-life might try to rob me.

As I turn to stumble toward a *Silkwood*-style erasure of last night's transgressions, the shiny golden key seems to call to me.

I pick up the key and feel the heft of it in my hand. The brass is cool to the touch, and the angled barrel displays the scars of age and use. It's definitely larger than any key I've ever seen—and it's not flat. It's sort of a triangle-ish thing with teeth on all three sides.

Weird.

I can't seem to put the key down, so I hold it in my right hand while I shuffle through the loose papers with my left.

Does that say "Last Will and Testament?"

I drop the key.

My eyes race over the words, and with each sentence my hands shake a little more.

My grandmother, a woman I've never met, is dead. But the thing that is flipping my beanie is that this is my disappearing dad's mother. She's dead and she left me her bookshop in some podunk town clinging to the shores of some Great Lake I've never heard of . . .

The cash is meant to help me settle my affairs—if only—and relocate to said podunk town. This stranger thinks (thought) that I would abandon my life to run some small-town bookstore?

I make no effort to stifle my laughter as I drop the papers and walk toward the bathroom, shaking my head.

The steam swirls around me while I scrub the shampoo into my cigarette-smoke-scented white-blonde hair. Another gift from slumming it with Shady Ben. Seems like the second time this month I ended up pity-kissing a rando in the smoke pit at a bar/party.

SPUTTER.

SILENCE.

"No. No. No. Please do not do this right now." I twist the turny knobs in the shower, rub the tile like a magic lamp, and pray to the shower gods to give me enough water to rinse the flipping shampoo out of my ey—

DELUGE.

Ice-cold water thunders out of the showerhead and blasts all sound and feeling from my world. I'm so shocked I can neither speak nor move. I gasp and suck in air as if that can counter the freezing fluid. Fortunately, I've played through this scene a few times and I know the water could stop again at any moment, so I bite the inside of my cheek to keep from screaming and thrust my head under the icy spray.

The water indeed ceases to grace me with its presence roughly sixty seconds later. Close enough.

Wrapping a towel around my shivering body, I run to the kitchenette to make some hot coffee.

No coffee.

That sounds about right.

I promised myself I'd stop at the Qwik Mart after the party last night and grab a few things.

Clearly that did not happen.

On the bright side, I didn't wake up in Shady Ben's shifty bed!

Time to get dressed and run down to that coffee shop where I work and see if I can get a pre-shift cup of wake-up juice.

CHAPTER 2

DON'T WORRY, I put all the lovely cash inside a nearly empty box of waffles in my freezer-ette and taped the key under my toilet tank. I actually stuck the key under the tank with a wad of freshly chewed gum. You didn't believe I had tape, did you?

Now that I'm rich I have to be more careful. Plus, if life in the foster system has taught me anything, that weird old dude will be back this afternoon to say "gotcha" or "oops" and take it all back.

Pushing open the door of Hot Kafka, I inhale the rich scent of waking up.

Dang it! I forgot to clean the whipped-cream stain off my uniform. Maybe I can slip into the bathroom before anyone sees me.

"Namaste, Mitzy!" Prayer hands and a blessed

head nod approach as the soundtrack of singing bowls reaches a crescendo.

Fan-flipping-tastic. The SUPERvisor is already on me. "Hey, Dean." If I still had long hair I could sweep it in front of my face and hide the stain as I run to the bathroom. However, two weeks ago, after I lost a drunken karaoke bet, I ended up with a cross between a Cardi B. pixie and a Betty White curl-bob. I refer to this as the "Bad Bet." Not my finest moment.

"Hey Mitzy, where ya headed?" He tilts his head with what I'm sure he thinks is concern.

Dean miraculously crosses the entire Saltillo-tile floor in seconds and now stands inches from my person.

"Just a quick trip to the restroom before my shift, Dean." I try to scoot past.

"Well that's the thing, Mitzy. Your shift started at 9:45 and it's already 10:00, and well, I'd just be super-pumped if you would take care of your personal business at home and show up on time and ready to work." Huge smile.

And there it is. SUPERvisor Dean is always super-pumped about something. I live for his life lessons. "Copy that, Dean. I'll just—"

"Oh boy, Mitzy. Is that a stain on your uniform? It's darkening your whole aura." Huge smile downgrades to miniscule grin as he gestures toward my Macbeth-sized spot.

I swat his unwelcome paw away from my boob area. "I'll just clean it up right quick and be ready to go."

"Well, gee whiz, Mitzy, I'm gonna have to get you a new shirt and dock that from your pay. I'm super-sorry about that, but we have to put our best face forward at the Hot Kafka. Our customers expect a certain vibe." He finishes with an emphatic nod and an attaboy fist pump.

I'm pretty sure our customers expect coffee without spit in it. I mean, if they wanted fancy coffee served by people in clean uniforms they'd march down the street to the chain store with the mood lighting and free Wi-Fi. Of course, I don't say any of this to Dean. I nod and smile.

As I watch Dean's peppy step take him to the Kokopelli-embellished stockroom door something dawns on me. Hey, wait one darn tootin' minute. I'm rich. I don't need this ridiculous job or this insanely positive SUPERvisor. I follow Dean into the stockroom and make my announcement. "I quit."

"Oh, hey now, Mitzy. Don't get your chakras out of alignment." He raises his hands like this is a robbery. "You'll be back in the black in no time. I'll only charge you my cost for the new uniform shirt. How's that sound?"

I'm sorry about this next part. Please skip ahead and pretend you don't see me do this. "Ya know what, Dean? Here's how it sounds!" I take off the stained shirt, throw it in his shocked face, and strut out of Hot Kafka into the unforgiving Arizona sun.

Too bad I didn't remember that I was wearing my skanky, greyish, holey bra BEFORE I made my statement. The strut would've been so much more impressive in a red lacey push-up thingy.

Instead I run home with my arms crossed over my chest, sweat trickling down my back, and a little muffin topping my skinny jeans.

Slamming my apartment door behind, I throw the deadbolt home.

Just when I finally learned the name of the place, too . . . so long, Hot Kafka. "We could've been Franz." I choke on my own pun as a loud and threatening knock assaults my door.

I hold my breath.

"I seen ya run in there, ya trollop."

That is Mr. Coleman. My landlord. Did you already guess that my rent is late—again?

"I'll be back in the morning with an eviction notice. Ya hear me?"

THUMP!

I jump as his fist connects with the door in one last frustrated punch.

A sudden need to explore lakes comes over me. I believe they were purported to be "great?"

So long Sedona!

I pack my stuff in a crummy ripped duffle bag and an old rucksack. In the movies there's always a framed picture that gets lovingly tucked in the top, but none of my pre-tragedy childhood trinkets survived the foster care system. And now I tend to move frequently; so keeping the load light is essential.

I put the cash in my boots, underwear, bra, and a bit in my wallet. Not exactly sure what to do with the key and not super committed to drug-mule-style hiding.

I have a collection of keys I "borrowed" from the homes where I was placed from eleven until I aged out, but this strange key feels different. This key was given to me. This key was a gift from an actual relative.

I opt for a chain.

I slip the "jewelry" under my shirt and wait for the cover of darkness. Now that I've got money, I don't want to waste any of my little pile of wealth on back rent. I mostly want to make a clean getaway and see what my key opens. It feels like a morbid game show.

"Mitzy Moon! Your long-lost grandmother is dead! Let's see what you've won!"

CHAPTER 3

I DON'T THINK THIS LOUD, smelly bus could possibly make any more stops! I mean, why in the wide world does a bus need to stop at an empty bench in a town with the same population as I have fingers?

No one boards. I'm as shocked as you are.

We lurch forward, and I force myself to breathe as shallowly as possible. The odor of diesel fumes, unwashed humanity, and day-old turkey sub—with a soupçon of stale cigarette smoke—is not something I want seeping into the depths of my lung tissue.

I wish I'd made some hatch marks on the bus seat to count the passing days, but it's more than two and less than a million. Finally, the sign for Pin Cherry Harbor welcomes me and promises an end to this *Groundhog Day* of a bus ride.

It's not a green and white metal sign like most

places. No ma'am, this town has a bespoke sign carved from wood and hand-painted with bunches of what can only be pin cherries in each corner.

The bus lurches to a stop with a screech of the brakes and a puff of exhaust. I step off, choke on the engine's haze, and walk to the sidewalk.

I immediately regret my decision to risk a cross-country migration.

No parade. No welcome wagon.

A typical relocation with all the familiar acid reflux and floating detachment.

I look up and down the street that seems to have fallen out of an old black-and-white movie. Nothing too appealing: Rex's Drugstore, a boarded up Montgomery Wards, an unnamed hardware store. But when my eyes fall on Myrtle's Diner the color floods in like a frame from Dorothy's Oz, and I feel the call of the fry.

My stomach growls as I cross the street. When I open the door the smells of grease and goodness hit me almost as hard as the seven sets of eyeballs.

I nod and slip into the nearest booth.

A server who bears the nametag "Tally" swoops in.

"Just passin' through, eh?" She nods, and her freshly dyed, flaming-red topknot reminds me of a cherry adorning a rather old sundae.

I could say "yes," place my order, and go about

my business, but . . . "No ma'am, I think I might stay. I'd like a cheeseburger, well done, with a side of fries. I'll take a bottle of hot sauce with that if you've got it. Oh, and a soda."

Tally's pen does not move. It hovers above the order pad like a super-slo-mo space shuttle docking.

"That's it for me," I add with a tip of my head and a slightly raised eyebrow above my folksy grin.

Tally mumbles something incoherent and hustles back to the kitchen as fast as her elderly legs can take her.

I swivel my head to scan the place for a possible "Myrtle."

All eyes, seven pairs, stare unblinkingly at me.

Including Tally and the cook, who both peer through the red Formica trim of the "orders-up" window.

I give another nod, turn back to my booth, and search diligently for nothing in my rucksack.

The silence reminds me of a country song where everyone can hear a pin drop, or an old saloon after the gun-slinging outlaw walks through the swinging doors. That's me. I guess there's a new sheriff in town and if they don't like it—

The front door of the diner whips open and the actual strong-jawed, clean-cut sheriff bursts through. Uniform freshly laundered. Check. Blonde hair neatly slicked back. Check.

Do I love a man in uniform? Check!

"This the gal here?" The broad-shouldered sheriff gestures toward me and scans the patrons.

I don't turn around, but I think it's safe to assume they all nod.

"Hey there, Miss. We have a strict policy on vagrants in Pin Cherry Harbor. So, I'll just get Tally to pack up your food to go and I'll give you a lift outta town. Sound good?"

I could pull out the will and maybe even brandish the key. Of course, I go another direction entirely. I stand up real slow, like it pains me to have to do it. I look down at the black and white linoleum squares, take a deep breath and look up at the sheriff. When I catch sight of his dreamy blue eyes my heart snaps out a few extra beats and I forget the smart-alec line I want to say. Instead I go with, "Aren't you a tall drink of water." To be fair, he's at least six-foot plus two or three inches.

He blushes profusely. The color only adds to his charm.

I smile wickedly as I remember my line. "I wasn't expecting such a formal welcome, Officer, but I appreciate you takin' time out of your busy day to make me feel so special." I step closer.

He sucks in a breath and tries to step back. I say "tries" because he catches the heel of one of his steel-toed boots on the toe of the other, stumbles, flails, and snags my arm as he falls backward.

Now, I'm no waif, but I'm smaller than him. So, he continues to tumble and I, of course, land smack dab on top of him.

A collective gasp rises from the diner.

I instantly make matters worse by saying, "Well, welcome to Pin Cherry yourself, Sheriff."

His angled jaw flexes and his muscular chest rises and falls rapidly beneath me. As his face shifts to a shade of red that surely puts the town's namesake to shame, I roll clear and offer him a hand.

He shakes his head vigorously, releasing the slicked-back hair so that it falls over his eye in an unintentionally sexy manner. He gets to his feet under his own power.

I notice his thumb depress the button on his radio—twice. In case you're not familiar, this is called "keying" your radio. As a film school dropout, I can tell you how we used to do this on the film set when we needed to respond to something that came over the headset but couldn't answer verbally because the cameras were rolling. I'm pretty sure I just saw the sheriff signal for help.

Tally attempts to hand me a Styrofoam container.

I wave it away and finally brandish the key. "I'll take that for here, Tally." I turn to show everyone the key. "And then I'll be opening up my bookstore if anyone needs a new summer read." My heart thumps rapidly in complete opposition to my false bravado.

A voice crackles over the radio. "Sheriff, you're needed urgently at headquarters."

Didn't I tell you?

Sheriff Too Hot To Handle scrapes his hair back into place, mumbles something under his breath, and practically runs out the door.

I grin stupidly and stare a little too long at his exit.

If one of my student films had been this riveting I never would've abandoned film school.

Tally returns with an honest-to-goodness plate, silverware, my soda, and a bottle of Tabasco that looks older than me.

I ease back into the booth and eat my burger like I got all the time in the world. The remaining customers trickle out—each one sliding me a hard side-eye as they pass.

Once the place clears of customers the cook saunters out and slips into the other side of my booth. His worn dungarees make a short squeak against the red vinyl.

He sizes me up, and I wonder if my bus-applied makeup and dry-shampooed hair will pass muster.

I size him up right back. He's old. Not creepy-crumbly old, but the kind of face that has a story tucked in every crease and eyes that still hold a little fire in their coffee-dark depths. His grey hair is buzzed short, but covers his head in a utilitarian fashion.

I nod.

He nods.

"I've got money," I say with a bit more indignation than I intend.

"I figured as much." His voice is rough as a Brillo Pad, but as comforting as a favorite chair. "So Myrtle left you her bookshop, eh?"

"Mmhmm," I say. I hope we're talking about the same Myrtle. It's especially confusing because I'm fairly certain I'm sitting in Myrtle's Diner, and it seems unlikely that there could be two Myrtles in town.

"You don't look much like her." He tilts his head. "Maybe around the eyes. She had those mischievous grey peepers." His gaze drifts off and a soft smile plays across his lips.

"Did you know my grandmother?"

"I figure I knew her better than you." He clenches his jaw.

"Fair enough."

"You got the gift, too?" His gaze narrows and he shifts in his seat.

I have no idea what he's talking about. Is the

bookstore the gift? And what does he mean by "too?" Is there some other person who inherited the shop? I swallow all those questions and go with, "I'm not sure what you mean?"

"Myrtle had visions. She called 'em premonitions. You get any of those?" He lifts his chin and waits.

And I thought Sedona was full of nutters. "Uh, nope. No visions here."

"Why'd you come?" He leans back and places both hands against the edge of the table.

Aw what the heck. I got nothing to lose, right? "My mother died when I was eleven, I never knew my father, and life in general has not worked out so great for me. I figured I might as well see what Pin Cherry Harbor has to offer."

He nods real slow and fixes me with a surprisingly gentle stare. "Burgers are on the house as long as you're in town." His eyes glisten as he whispers, "She would've wanted that." He slaps the silver-flecked white table once, nods, and returns to the kitchen.

I walk to the counter and peer through the orders-up window. "You never answered my question. How well did you know my grandmother?"

He works his jaw back and forth and I can see he's working hard to stuff his emotions back down where they belong. "Name's Odell."

That name rings a bell. I remember reading it on the bus when I was reviewing the will. It said, *To Odell Johnson, who has always had my heart, I leave my share of Myrtle's Diner*. I smile knowingly and repeat my question. "So, how well did you know my grandmother?"

"I'll answer that one on our second date." A sly smile tugs at the corner of his mouth and crinkles his cheek.

"Fair enough." I walk toward the door and toss over my shoulder, "I don't suppose you can point me toward the bookshop, can you?"

He chuckles, and a metal spatula scrapes across the grill before he answers, "Down Main Street, to your left. Can't miss it."

If I had a quarter for every time someone had given me "can't miss it" directions, I'd be a— Oh, that's right. I am.

CHAPTER 4

WELL, I'LL BE A MONKEY'S UNCLE! You actually can't miss it. Right on the corner of Main and First. I lean back and shade my eyes against the mid-morning sun. "Wow!" I look around to see if anyone heard my exclamation, but the streets are devoid of walkers, and the old truck sputtering down the road can't hear a thing.

I walk down the side of the massive three-story brick building and run my hand along the rough red-brown surface. I catch my breath as I come face to face with the "great lake" mentioned in the documents, which provided much-needed entertainment on the bus. "Wow!" I say again.

I've never seen this much water in my entire life. The sheer volume is obscene. A flash flood in the desert during the brief monsoon season is a dripping faucet compared to this lush, liquid paradise. The sun sparkles off the water, birds swoop and dive overhead, the cool breeze flutters my hair, and—

"Hey there, you gonna open up or not?"

I swallow my awe and turn to see one of the pairs of eyes from the diner posted up outside my bookshop. I guess I'm gonna open.

I slip the chain with the key over my head as I walk toward my first customer. "I'm Mitzy. What's your name?" The woman looks about fifty or sixty. I'm not that great at guessing people's ages. Her black denim pants, Styx T-shirt, and biker boots say fifty-ish, but her severe grey pixie and lined face whisper an older tale.

"I didn't come for chit-chat, girlie. Are ya opening or not?"

So much for Midwestern charm.

The eight-foot solid wood door that bars my entry to the bookshop is a work of art. I don't have time to inspect the careful craftsmanship that adorns the massive piece with delicate and detailed carving—there is too much sighing and foot tapping behind me. I run my fingers along the edge opposite the hefty iron hinges and locate the cleverly concealed opening that contains the "plug." Yes, I did learn how to pick locks from a delinquent older foster brother. But even he couldn't have popped this cherry. His gross term, not mine. I slide my triangular key into the lock and turn. I don't hear a click so much as I "feel" the lock open. I actually think I felt the whole store awaken. And I realize that sounds as weird as it—well, sounds.

I pull the heavy, ornate door open and have to physically arm-bar the patron from entering before me. It's my shop. I want to be the first to walk in.

No Chit-chat exhales loudly.

I feel around on the left and right for the light switches. Nothing. Goose egg. Nada.

"Oh for cryin' out loud," exclaims No Chit-chat as she bustles past me and disappears into the store.

I gaze around in the dust-filtered window-light and breathe in the scent of worlds. I imagine a short film that will take place within—

LIGHTS.

A massive chandelier flashes to life above me and I gasp.

I crane my neck to take in the impossibly voluminous space. The building did not look anywhere near this large from the outside. There are three stories of bookshelves. All the way from the richly carpeted floor to the gleaming tin-plated ceiling.

A balcony curves from one side of the second floor to the other, passing through a lovely loft/mezzanine in the back.

I drop my bags to the floor and hop-step over

the "No Admittance" chain, run up the wrought-iron circular staircase to the open-plan second floor, and take in the mesmerizing view back toward the rows of slumped-glass windows. Dust floating in the air seems to ride on a gentle breeze down to the bookcases in their thick, stoic rows on the first floor.

"You need me to run to the bank and get the drawer money?"

Oh crap, I completely forgot about my customer. I hurry down the stairs, trip a little, catch myself on the railing, stumble over my bags, and skitter to a halt in front of No Chit-chat. "Why would I need drawer money? And why would I send you to get it if I did, Mrs.—?"

"Nope. No 'Mrs.' Never wrapped that noose around my neck. Everybody calls me 'Twiggy.'"

Twiggy. Hmmm. Now that would be the perfect name for Fat Carol. "All right. Can I help you find something today, Twiggy?"

"You can't even find the lights, doll. And to answer one of your many earlier questions, you need drawer money to put in the cash register." She puts up a finger, capped by a close-clipped nail, to shush me and continues, "You send me to get it 'cuz I been workin' part-time for your Grams during high season since she had this old brewery converted into a bookstore."

I glance around the utterly empty bookshop

and nod and smile. "Well, how is it that you have access to my grandmother's—rather—my bank account?"

"Are you always this thick, or did you hit your head when you tackled the sheriff?"

I clench my jaw to prevent a stream of unlady-like phrases from spilling out of my beautiful mouth. "Humor me," I manage to say.

"Tilly's been the teller at the bank practically since the money came by stagecoach. She knows me. She knew your Grams. I walk in, ask for the drawer money, and she hands it over." Twiggy shakes her head like she's ashamed of me. "If I went in there and ask Tilly for $10,000 in small bills she'd laugh and call the sheriff. Understand?"

I barely understand a single word, but I'm not going to give her the satisfaction. I'll refer you to a corollary to the first rule of foster care: never show weakness. "I understand that the only thing standing between me and an empty bank account is a sheriff who can't manage to stand on his own two feet. Oh, and apparently Tilly simultaneously works at the bank and the diner." I give her a "take that" smirk.

Twiggy looks heavenward and invokes my grandmother. "Myrtle Isadora Johnson Linder Duncan Willamet Rogers, if I didn't think so highly of you I'd run this scrawny idiot out of town before sunset."

All I heard was that she thinks I'm skinny. Nice. Oh, that and the fact that my grandmother had at least five husbands . . .

"Tally works at the diner. Tilly works at the bank. They're sisters. Folks say their parents named each of the kids after the town where he or she was conceived. Now I'm not saying it's an appropriate system, but the oldest sister got made in Tillamook, Wisconsin, and goes by Tilly. The youngest got made in Tallahassee, Florida, and goes by Tally, and the brother in the middle got cooked up in Toledo, Ohio, and goes by—"

"Toley," I blurt.

"What the heck kinda name is Toley? No, wise-acre, he goes by Ledo."

I don't believe her for one second. I don't think she liked me stealing her punch line, so she made up the bit about the brother. Regardless, apparently this ornery spinster is my employee, and since I know less than nothing about this place I better make nice. "I'll make a note of those names. Now, would you please walk on over to the bank and get the drawer money. And maybe you can show me around the shop when you get back. Okay?"

Twiggy strides toward the front door and calls back, "Sure enough. I'll show you around the museum and the apartment, too. I s'pose you'll need a place to stay—if you're stayin'." Just before the door closes she adds, "Don't mess with Pyewacket. He ain't a fan of strangers, you know."

The massive door bangs shut behind her, and I make a mental note to get some kind of spring or shock for the unwieldy thing. It's strangely out of place in the brewery-turned-bookshop. The door is intricately decorated with symbols and figures that whisper of faraway places—perhaps my grandmother was a traveler. My gaze returns to the shelves and shelves of books. Reading was my escape from the pain and loss that followed my mother's death. Books contained the only true friends I'd ever known. I smile broadly and close my eyes. I can almost feel the dust in the air, but I inhale deeply regardless of the atoms of paper I'm surely taking in. As I breathe in the energy flowing through the room, there's a noise like someone scratching on metal.

I pop open my eyes and walk toward the sound. There must be a side or rear door. I wander into the back room where Twiggy disappeared earlier and the volume increases.

An illuminated "Exit" sign spills red light into the dim space. As I near the door the scraping becomes clearer. It is definitely an animal. My heart skips a beat. What if my grandmother left me a puppy? I slowly push open the door so I don't hit the hopefully adorable puppy.

Imagine my shock and disappointment when instead of a cuddly bundle of cuteness, I discover a dog-sized alley cat that appears to be half bobcat and half demon! Oh, and it has something nasty in its pointy-toothed mouth. Great! I was hoping to come face to face with a dead mouse today.

I wave my arms to shoo the cat away, but she— or maybe he—I didn't check under the hood, so let's go with "it." It drops the dead thing on the step and squirts past me into the bookstore in a blur of tan fur and tufted ears that almost knocks me off my feet.

Pyewacket, I assume. Nice to make your acquaintance.

Before my brain can send the "give chase" signal, I inexplicably bend down to get a closer look at the leavings.

"Son of a—" I won't repeat what I actually say. In fact, I won't even tell you what's lying on the step. I run into the bookstore screaming unrepeatables at the cat, who I'm now sure is Pyewacket, while I search for a spoon (ew) or tweezers (yuck) or a dustpan. All I can find are chopsticks.

I demand that the cat get out of my bookshop, and to my great surprise, as I open the side door the demon-spawn feline rockets into the alley.

I pick up the "thing" on the step with the chopsticks and fiercely fight my gag reflex as I shuffle-run toward the dumpster at the end of the alley.

My fingers are shaking.

The thing is slipping.

I am less than a foot from the finish line and my arm is poised to dump and run.

A car turns down the alley.

BWAAP. BWAAP.

Two quick hoots from a siren. Hooray.

Red and blue lights swirl on and off, filling the alleyway with an unwelcome, and wholly misleading, party-like atmosphere.

I slowly turn toward the intrusion.

"I thought that was you," he says.

Sheriff Too Hot To Handle is back for seconds.

"Freeze."

Did he just pull a gun on me?

"Don't take another step." He inches closer. "And drop the— Is that an eyeball?"

Clearly the sheriff is not as thoughtful as me. I'm sorry you had to hear it that way.

I nod and smile. What else can I do?

"Drop the eyeball," he repeats. "And step away from the body."

CHAPTER 5

WAIT, WHAT? DID HE SAY "BODY?"

In the confusion, I fail to follow orders and instead turn to see the alleged body. At that exact moment the freaktastic feline Pyewacket leaps out of the dumpster.

Our local jumpy lawman pulls his trigger.

He misses psycho-kitty, but the bullet ricochets off the dumpster and—you guessed it—grazes my shoulder. I scream, drop the icky thing and the chopsticks, and fall on my rump in the alley.

Luckily, Twiggy sees my entire catastrophic embarrassment and delivers exactly what I need most. An earsplitting cackle.

I grab my shoulder and shout, "He shot me! You shot me, you crazy hick cop!" Warm crimson fluid oozes between my fingers, and the alley seems to spin like a merry-go-round.

"Did she call you a hiccup?" Twiggy says to the sheriff through peals of laughter.

All of a sudden her jocularity comes to an abrupt halt. "Is that a body?" Her voice is an octave higher and the laughter noticeably absent.

"I caught her red-handed. Right here, plain as day, trying to dispose of the body." He picks up his radio and calls in something about a 187, some other numbers, and an afterthought about an injured perp.

From rich to perp in less than a week. This must be how Willie Nelson felt. I know I'll probably rot in a cell in this one-horse town, but when Sheriff Too Hot To Handle walks toward me and pulls out his handcuffs, all I can think is how good it feels to be guilty.

"Stand up real slow—um, what's your name?"

I stand. "What's yours, Sheriff? I can't keep calling you Too Hot To Handle." I smile and wobble unsteadily.

He flushes handsomely and his strong jaw twitches as though he's stifling a chuckle. "Name?" he repeats in his "all business" voice.

"Mine's Mitzy Moon, Officer." I hold out one wrist.

"I'll need both hands for the cuffs, Miss Moon."

"I thought you'd never ask." I wink, but as soon as I remove my right hand from my injured left shoulder the blood flows, the stinging resumes, and I faint.

Regaining consciousness in the ambulance, my eyes struggle to focus. The sheriff angles over me with concern, and just a few strands of enticingly out-of-place hair fall over his eye and beg to be touched.

The paramedic shines a bright penlight in each of my eyes and announces, "She's coming around, Harper."

The man named "Harper" leans in.

I smile up at the intense blue-grey eyes and whisper, "What's your first name, Harper?"

The sheriff exhales, leans back, and replies, "It's Erick. But you can call me Sheriff Harper."

I attempt to lift my right arm to give him a proper handshake, and that's when I feel the hand-cuff clamping my wrist to the gurney.

"Mitzy Moon, you're under arrest for the murder of Cal Duncan. You have the right to re-main silent. Anything . . . "

My ears ring just like the victims in the after-math of a concussion grenade in a B-movie. Mur-der? I thought throwing my uniform shirt at SUPERvisor Dean was daring and reckless. I've never murdered anything in my life. Except possibly a molten-chocolate lava cake.

As the ambulance comes to an abrupt halt and the paramedic jumps out to slide the gurney to the ground, I get a bright idea. "I want to speak to my lawyer."

"I'll call him for you while they stitch you up. What's his name?" Sheriff Harper pulls out his pen and notepad.

I smile sheepishly. "No idea. I thought I'd call the guy who delivered—" That's the exact moment I remember that I have wads of cash stuffed into my undergarments. Oops.

"Do you mean Silas Willoughby? Your grandmother's attorney?"

"Mmhmm." I nod and smile. "I'd like to speak to him before I see the doctor."

The sheriff gives me a highly suspicious look and lowers his notepad. "Are you refusing medical treatment?" He puts a hand on the gurney. "Hold up, medic," he says to the attendant.

"Not so much refusing as postponing."

"Take her into One," the doctor commands.

He continues to hold the gurney and replies, "She's refusing treatment, Doc."

Boy that Sheriff Harper is a real stickler.

"Jump off the gurney and have a seat in the waiting room, Miss. You'll change your mind when the wound starts bleeding again." The doctor tosses me an exasperated eye roll. "And it will start bleeding again." She hustles off to attend to other matters before I can reply.

Sheriff Harper unlocks one side of the handcuffs from the gurney and locks it around his own wrist.

A tingle of anticipation slides down my spine. You have my attention.

"Dispatch, can you send Deputy Paulsen down to County? I've got a babysitting job for her."

Rude.

"Oh, and get Willoughby on the horn. Tell him Isadora's granddaughter is being charged with the murder of Cal Duncan."

"10-4, Sheriff."

"You can't possibly believe I murdered anyone." I stare at the sheriff in shock. "I'd be covered in blood spatter, for one thing, and—"

He points at my shirt.

"That's my blood. From when you shot me!" I shake my head and chew the inside of my cheek. "This is entrapment. You framed me."

"Do you want to head over to the station for questioning?" He raises an eyebrow.

Butterflies in my tummy take note of his sexy arched brow and intense stare and flutter mercilessly. "What about my arm?" I gulp some air and command my stomach to behave.

"You refused medical treatment."

"I didn't. I asked for my attorney."

"Then we can't discuss the case." He shakes his head in exasperation and smiles. "You can't have it both ways, Miss Moon."

Before I can enjoy his satisfied grin, our intense flirtation is interrupted.

"Sorry it took me so long, Sheriff. That Johan Olafsson was driving his tractor right down Main Street again." The short, squat deputy sizes me up. "This the killer?"

"Alleged killer," I interject.

"She's got a mouth on her, eh? Want me to quiet her down, Sheriff?" She rocks back and forth on her tiny feet in a way that reminds me of one of those punching bags with all the sand in the bottom. The kind that kids knock down but the character keeps rolling back up.

I don't like the ilk of this deputy—not one bit.

"There's no need for that, Paulsen." He transfers the other half of my handcuffs from his inviting wrist to the ample deputy's limb. "Take her into the waiting area and keep your eyes peeled for Willoughby."

"Figures she'd lawyer up. The guilty always

do." She snarls her lip up and jerks toward me like a playground bully.

I don't flinch. One of the first things I learned in foster care was to stand my ground with bullies. I still got the crap beat out of me pretty regularly, but at least I went down fighting.

Paulsen tugs me along behind her as though I'm a bad puppy and directs me, rather roughly, into a dusty-rose vinyl-covered chair.

"Gimme a holler on the squawk box when Silas arrives." Sheriff Harper tips his chin and leaves me to stew with my babysitter.

She nods and picks at her teeth with a toothpick that seems to materialize out of thin air.

Now that my tasty distraction has exited, I notice the antiseptic odor and the chill in the air. I don't like hospitals. Never have. I reach to pull the edge of my shirt down with the handcuffed wrist.

Paulsen instantly yanks her hand. "Give me a reason, scumbag." She massages the handle of her gun and narrows her gaze.

Seems like now would be the wrong time to mention how badly I need to pee.

CHAPTER 6

You know that scene in the movie when the music swells and the hero rushes in with a dramatic flourish to save the day? This is nothing like that.

"Over here, Silas." Deputy Paulsen lifts her pudgy hand from her gun for a moment and gives a quick two-finger wave.

Silas Willoughby shuffles down the linoleum corridor with absolutely no sense of urgency. His wrinkled brown suit, mystery-sauce-stained tie, and dilapidated briefcase mumble of a forgotten era. Picture present day Nick Cage in a remake of *Death of a Salesman*.

"Mizithra." He nods.

"Silas." I shrug my wounded arm and nod my head toward the injury, while fluttering the fingers on the handcuffed wrist.

He straightens, harrumphs into his mustache, and seems to gain six inches in height. "Deputy Paulsen, remove the restraints from my client. She is a business owner in the community and not a flight risk."

To my utter stupefaction, Deputy Paulsen works her fat little hand into her snug polyester pocket, pulls out her key, and unlocks the handcuffs.

I rub my wrist and stare at Silas with my mouth hanging open.

He extends a hand, which I gladly take. As he gently pulls me to my feet he places his other hand over my gunshot wound and murmurs something under his breath.

"I don't believe you'll require any sutures, Mizithra. Allow me to convey you to the bookshop, so you have a moment to freshen up before our visitation with Sheriff Harper."

I nod but can't seem to find the mental capacity to smile. I'm too busy staring at my shoulder. There's nothing more than a scratch. The stinging is gone, and the wound is no longer bleeding.

Mr. Willoughby drives me back to the bookstore in his mint condition 1908 Model T. The seats show some wear and the steering wheel has two smooth indentations that cradle his hands, but other than that the vehicle looks like it rolled off the assembly line yesterday.

He parks on the street and I slide out of the car. As I walk up to the door I look at the sign. "Bell, Book & Candle Bookshop." I honestly don't remember seeing that sign this morning. Maybe I did hit my head when I tumbled all over Sheriff Too Hot To Handle—I mean, Erick.

"The key, Mizithra."

"Oh, right." I fumble around under my shirt and extract the key, which has snagged on a one hundred dollar bill from my bra. "Oops." I tug the bill loose and shove it back into my "B" cup.

Mr. Willoughby shakes his head twice before his shoulders return to their normal curve of disappointment.

I put the key in, but there's no "open" sound or feeling. I tug the handle and the door opens. "I left Twiggy in charge," I offer with a shrug.

"You powder your nose and I'll wait in the stacks." He walks into the rows of bookshelves at the front of the shop.

I wander around and try to locate my bags.

An additional instruction floats over the shelves. "Do try to find something other than skinny jeans."

The way he enunciates "skinny jeans" makes them sound like poisonous snakes.

"I put your stuff in the apartment," announces Twiggy.

"And that would be . . . ?"

"Up the stairs, through the Rare Books Loft, tilt the candle next to the copy of *Saducismus Triumphatus* and you're in."

"Maybe you could show me?"

She doesn't respond.

"I have blood all over my hands. I wouldn't want to get that on the candle or the *Saducismus*."

A heavy sigh followed by clomping footfalls herald the approach of Twiggy.

"This way, Your Highness." We twist our way upstairs and through the rows of carefully aligned oak reading tables, each with a lovely brass lamp topped by a thick, green glass shade.

Despite my irritation with Twiggy's curt manner, the secret door does not fail to impress.

"Thanks."

Twiggy exhales and stomps back down the staircase.

I run my hand along the edge of the bookcase door and grin maniacally. My grandmother, who some people in town call Myrtle and others call Isadora, is—was . . . I wish I could've known her. I think she would get me, and vice versa.

After I complete a quick treasure hunt and pull all the hundreds out of my clothes, boots, and undergarments, I stuff the bills under the mattress. I don't know. I'm spitballing at this point.

I whip off my shirt, wash the blood from my hands and arm, and slip on a clean T-shirt. I glance down at the shirt. A cat spilling a cup of coffee with the tagline, "I Do What I Want."

Not quite the right message for an interrogation.

Pulling that one off, I dig through my crap duffle bag for an attitude-free shirt. The best I can find is a blue shirt with images of cassette tapes, huge old cellular phones, CDs, pagers, and other "dead tech." It doesn't have a tagline and it's all I've got. I hope no one gets the joke.

I exit the apartment and tilt the candle back to level. The secret bookcase door slides shut. Sweet! I pitter-patter down the steps.

Silas Willoughby glances up. His face says "not pleased" in at least five languages.

I shrug.

"Do you have identification?"

"Yep." I pat my back pocket. "It's in my pocket," I hastily add, in case he thinks I think my rear end is identification.

"Of course it is," he mumbles as he shuffles out the front door.

CHAPTER 7

THE SHERIFF'S STATION looks exactly like I imagine it should. A touch of Sheriff Valenti from Roswell with a heaping helping of Sheriff Andy Taylor from Mayberry.

Sheriff Harper walks out from his office.

Oh my, I need to add a slice of sex on toast to that description. "Hi, Erick."

"I asked you to call me Sheriff Harper, Miss Moon." While his words say "no," his grin says "maybe."

Silas steps on my witty reply. "Sheriff Harper, you cannot possibly believe that my client would take the life of Cal Duncan. She's hardly been in town long enough to make the man's acquaintance. What possible motive would she have to dispatch a perfect stranger?"

"Silas, you know as well as I do that Cal is this woman's grandfather. I wouldn't call that a perfect stranger."

Once again, I find my jaw flapping in the breeze. A grandfather! A week ago I was a poor orphan and now—now, I'm still an orphan. My relatives are dropping like flies. I guess I'm not poor, though. However, I am being accused of murder . . .

"Follow me, Miss Moon."

Sheriff Harper walks toward the back of the station and I eagerly follow. I make no effort to keep my eyes above the waist. If this is the last fine man I'm going to see before they send me up the river, I don't want to miss a thing.

He pulls out my chair and takes the one opposite.

"Miss Moon, what were you doing in that alley this morning?"

I open my mouth, but Silas places a firm hand on my arm. "You are not required to answer, Mizithra."

I ignore the odd heat of his fingers on my skin. "I'm happy to answer, and let's agree that you'll call me Mitzy from now on."

A pained exhale escapes Mr. Willoughby's person. His hand drops to his side. "As you wish, Mitzy."

"Well, Erick, I was disposing of the thing that

Pyewacket dropped on my back step. I barely looked at it, and I never saw a body until you pulled up and shot me."

"By 'thing' are you referring to the eyeball?"

I gag a little. "Yes."

"When did you arrive in Pin Cherry Harbor?"

"About five minutes before you walked in the diner and pulled me into that horizontal embrace." I nod with a hint of "game on."

"Can anyone confirm that, Miss Moon?"

"There were at least seven people in the diner. I'm sure one of them saw what happened."

He doesn't take the bait.

"What I'm asking, Miss Moon, is if anyone can confirm that you arrived in Pin Cherry this morning?"

Touché, Erick. Touché.

"I'm sure my client can produce her bus ticket, Sheriff. I assume that will suffice?" Silas pushes his chair back.

I straighten up and smile. Yeah. That should suffice. I could get used to having a lawyer.

"We're waiting on the medical examiner to confirm time of death, but if Miss Moon can verify her arrival as of this morning, I feel confident once we check her alibi we can clear her of the charges. I'm no expert, but that body—"

I hastily put up a hand. "Please don't finish that sentence, Erick."

He tilts his head and nods. "It's Sheriff Harper, Miss Moon."

"Come along, Mitzy." Silas wiggles my chair impatiently.

I stand and nod my farewell.

"Don't leave town, Miss Moon."

"I wouldn't dream of it, Erick." I get a little flush of tingles every time I say his name.

"Deputy Paulsen will have some papers for you to sign, Silas." He reaches out and shakes my lawyer's hand. "Thanks for comin' in."

Deputy Paulsen glares at me and picks her teeth with her pinky fingernail. "Sheriff tell you to stick close?"

I frown. "I own the bookshop. I'm not planning on going anywhere."

"That's right," she adds with a nod.

Silas ignores her completely, reads through the document on the proffered clipboard, and signs with an impressive flourish.

I lean in and admire his work. "Nice signature. You study calligraphy?"

"A person's name is a thing of beauty. A unique talisman. It deserves to be honored, Mitzy."

The tone with which he utters my nickname is

not lost on me. I shrug sheepishly and walk out of the station.

On the short ride back to the bookshop Silas doesn't volunteer any information about Cal Duncan, so I inquire, "Was Cal really my grandfather?"

Silas nods.

"Well, if Odell Johnson was her first husband then Cal Duncan—" I quickly review the order of her many surnames "—must've been her third. Right?"

He nods again.

"What's going on? What aren't you telling me?"

He takes a deep breath, lets it out slowly, and swallows. "It's not my place to say."

Can you believe this guy? It's been a heckuva day and I'm in no mood for games. "Everyone else is dead, Silas. It has to be your place. I've already been accused of murdering my own grandfather today. How much worse can things get?"

His shoulders stoop under some invisible weight and his jaw muscles tense. "Everyone else is not dead."

My mind goes into a tailspin. Thoughts are whirring around fast and furious. Holy crap! I have a sister or maybe a brother. I've always thought I would be a cool big sis—

"Your father is alive."

CHAPTER 8

DID I FAINT? I pinch myself. Ow! Apparently I did not faint. Another movie classic fails to deliver. My father is alive. Why has no one mentioned this since I arrived in Pin Cherry Harbor? Clearly everyone knows who my father is—everyone except me. Don't worry, I ask the obvious question. "Who's my father?"

"I can inform you his name is Jacob Duncan, but I'm afraid I can't say another word without acquiring his express permission." Silas squares his shoulders and turns off the sputtering engine.

"What? Has he refused to have anything to do with me? Is he ashamed of me? Is that why he ditched my mom after he knocked her up?" At least seventeen more questions zip around inside my head, but Silas refuses to answer me or even make eye contact, so whatever the reason that my dad won't acknowledge me—it must be pretty rotten.

I step out of the car and slam the tiny Model T door within an inch of its life. "Never mind. I didn't need him when my mom died. I didn't need him when they carted me off to foster care. I didn't need him when I ran away at seventeen and made it on my own." I choke back tears and shout at Silas and the rest of Pin Cherry, "I sure as heck don't need him now that I'm rich."

Silas makes no move to comfort me. Not that I expect him to, but I do see him flinch. Somehow that small victory satisfies me. I run inside the bookshop, up the stairs, and into my secret apartment.

As the bookcase slides shut behind me the tears flood down my cheeks.

I flop face down on the bed and punch my fist into a pillow until my arm shakes with fatigue. The tears are thick and the snot is thicker. This is a solid, ugly cry.

REOW! HISS!

I may have peed myself a little. My tears instantly cease as I whip around to locate the source of the commotion. "How did you get in here, Pyewacket?"

"Ree-ooow!" His back arches in an unfriendly pose.

"If that's meant to be an answer, I've got nothin', buddy."

"Oh, you'll understand his every sound before you know it."

I'm sorry to say I definitely pee myself this time. I spin around to confront this new intruder and my eyes nearly pop out of my head. The blood drains from my face and I'm sure I must be white as a—

"Were you going to say ghost, honey?"

The apparition floating in the middle of my apartment chuckles and clutches her many strands of pearls in amusement.

Now I faint.

A warm, rough tongue licks my cheek, but before I can get too excited sharp pointy teeth bite my earlobe. "Ow!" I swat at the carnivorous Pyewacket, but his cat-like—oh, that seems redundant—his reflexes easily put him out of reach before I can connect.

"Don't take it out on Pye. He just wants you to wake up so we can get acquainted. All caracal are intuitive, but his gift has always seemed abnormally strong. He's been quite protective of me ever since I won him in an off-the-books Scrabble game. His previous owner was a nasty piece of work. Poor little Pye was half-starved when I tucked him in my Marc Jacobs bag. I raised him from a cub, you know."

I sit up nice and slow. I scoot away from the swirling-misty ghost woman and press my back up against the solid wood frame of the four-poster bed.

"Mitzy, darling, I'm so sorry I didn't have the pleasure of meeting you in the flesh. Obviously you're in the flesh, but I'm a little, shall we say, insubstantial?"

Her laughter fills the room with love, and my terrified heart swells in spite of the primal fear. "Grams?"

"Who else?" She spins around and curtsies.

"You look so young. Silas said you were sixty-five when you passed."

"A lady never tells her age." Another chorus of chuckles. "One of the perks of being newly dead. I get to pick my 'look', and I went with circa thirty-five-year-old Isadora. Those early years with Cal and the baby were some of my best. And being buried in a vintage Marchesa didn't hurt!" She swishes back and forth to show off her burgundy silk-and-tulle ball gown.

"Is this real?" I press my hand against the floor and search the room for a clock. I'm fresh out of "Inception" tops so I'm not sure how to prove I'm not inside my own dream.

"If this is a dream, Mitzy, I don't ever want to wake up. You're exactly as beautiful and amazing as I knew you would be."

"You said 'the baby.' Do you mean my dad? Jacob?"

"Ah yes, that's why I'm here." Her mood darkens for a moment and she mumbles, "Silas and his rules."

"Silas said he wouldn't tell me anything without Jacob's permission."

"Well, Jacob is going to have a hard time enforcing his rules beyond the veil!" She crosses her arms and shakes her head.

"Silas said—"

"Silas can kiss my ample behind! That man never took proper advantage of me when he had the chance, and I'm not going to let him interfere with my afterlife."

And there it is. I just figured out where I get my trollop gene. Gram Gram is a little skanky!

"Easy honey, there's a thick line between 'empowered woman of means' and 'skank.'" She raises an eyebrow and nods.

"Can you read minds? Is that a ghost thing?"

She chews her perfectly drawn coral lip for a second. "I don't think it's mind reading. It just is. It seems like everything is energy, and now I'm connected to that energy in a different way. I'd say it feels more like there's no boundary between your thoughts and my thoughts. Does that make sense, dear?"

"Kinda." I shrug. Who am I to say what makes sense? I'm talking to a ghost.

She smiles and swirls closer. "Let me tell you about Jacob."

I grin and hug my knees to my chest.

She covers everything from his first tooth to his first day at college, before a dark cloud seeps into her energy. "When he dropped out of college and spent all his time with that Navy reject Darrin MacIntyre . . . " She presses her hand to her heart. "That's when Cal cut Jacob out of the will. How was he to know what would happen?"

"What? What happened?"

"Well, I hate to admit it, but Cal and I spoiled your father something fierce. So when the easy money stopped and Cal offered him an honest job, your father continued to take advantage of Cal's generosity. Eventually, he was fired and that's when things took a turn— He and that good-for-nothing Darrin cooked up a dangerous scheme."

"Like a pyramid scheme? Like multi-level marketing?" I lean forward.

"I wish, dear. No, I'm afraid they decided to rob one of those big box stores on Black Friday."

"Did they get caught?"

"Oh, that's not the half of it." She sighed and flickered. "The robbery went sideways and the store manager got shot. Now, I still don't believe Jacob did it, but that Darrin testified against him and your father went to prison for murder and armed robbery."

"*Holy Foley*! No wonder Silas didn't want to tell me."

"Don't blame Silas, dear. When your father found out about you he swore every member of the family to silence. He thought your mom was doing a great job raising you and he didn't want his mistakes to screw up your life."

"But she died when I was eleven and—"

"He told us nothing would be worse for you than having a convict for a father. Putting you in my will was my final rebellion. I never agreed with him, but I felt some kind of obligation while I was alive. He'd had such a hard life in prison."

"Had? Is he out of prison? Where is he? I want to meet him!" I get to my feet and pace. Part of me wants to meet him, at least. The other part kind of wants to yell at him and pound my fists against his chest—in the rain—like a Nicholas Sparks movie.

"Slow down, dear. Silas will get permission from Jacob, and then you can go and meet him. Last I heard he was down south somewhere. Seems like it might have been Chicago or Minneapolis."

My shoulders droop. "I can't leave town."

"Nonsense, dear. Twiggy and Pye can hold down the fort for a couple days."

"No, it's not that I don't *want* to leave town. I *can't*. I'm a suspect in Cal's murder."

Isadora's smile fades and her eyes fill with sadness and loss, or perhaps it's shock. The ghost of grandmothers past disapparates and Pyewacket hisses menacingly.

And . . . scene.

CHAPTER 9

I'M NOT CERTAIN if Grams left because of my implication in Cal's murder or if she received a summons from the other side, but either way I'm not waiting for anyone's permission on anything. I've made up my mind. I'm going to talk to my father.

Bounding down the stairs two at a time, I blindly trip over the chain at the bottom.

As I'm untangling myself and checking to make sure I didn't split open my skull, the dulcet tones of Twiggy's cackle reach my ears.

"You aren't exactly coordinated, eh? Seems like I've seen you on your hind end more than your feet today." Additional chuckles punctuate her observation.

"What's this stupid chain up for anyway? I don't care if people go up and down the stairs." I reach for the hook, but Twiggy's strong hand beats me to the clasp.

"You'll care if someone walks off with a book worth two hundred thousand dollars. Then you'll care." She does not remove her hand from the chain.

"You can't be serious!" I glance up the circular staircase and shake my head in disbelief.

"I realize you don't know me that well, doll, but I don't 'kid.'" Twiggy tilts her helmet of grey hair and crosses her arms over her square torso.

"If they're all so valuable, why aren't they in a museum or something?"

She makes a sweeping gesture to indicate the bookshop. "Behold 'something.' Once a month your Grams opens up the Rare Books Loft and every one of those little green-glass desk lamps shines on a rare tome that someone made reservations to view— months in advance."

"Do they pay for the reservation?" Little cash-register bells ding in my head.

"Naw. She only allows scholarly research, not looky-loos."

So much for my fleeting plans to take over the world with my rare-books money. "Hey, I need to do some research. Do we have old newspapers in here?"

"It's a bookshop not a library." Twiggy rolls her dark-brown eyes.

"I want to look into my dad's case. Grams seems pretty certain he's innocent and—"

Twiggy takes a big step back and stares at me like my head's on upside down. "I thought you never met Isadora? And who told you about your dad?"

Oops. I didn't think this through. I can't exactly tell her I've been chatting with my dead grandmother's ghost . . . First I'm a suspect in a murder and now I'm talking to dead people? I mean, this woman already thinks I'm uncoordinated and mildly incompetent. Do I want her assuming I'm a full on wack job?

"Is it the gift? She never thought it was hereditary. Your dad never . . . She wound up believing it was something she learned from the books."

Twiggy's rambling doesn't seem to be directed at me, but she sounds like she might be able to handle the truth. When in doubt . . .

I take a deep breath and launch into my tale. "I'm not sure how to explain this, Twiggy. I don't want you to think I'm insane or seeing things, but my grandmother's ghost appeared to me up in the apartment and told me all about the robbery and the murder charges." I swallow and wait.

Twiggy smacks the heels of her hands together as though I just gave her the answer to a riddle she'd been working on for months. "I knew it! If anyone could find a way back it would be Isadora. I bet you ten to one that Silas had something to do with this. He spends entirely too much time in that Rare Books Loft." She nods and paces in a circle. "I'd say I can't believe it, but I can. I absolutely can!"

This is going far better than I could've imagined.

Twiggy stops suddenly and glances left and right. "Is she here right now?"

I scrunch up my face and look down at the ground. "She sort of beamed out when I mentioned that I was accused of Cal's murder."

"Oh, hells bells, doll. You broke her heart. Cal was still alive when she crossed over. If she's trapped on our side she might not know . . ." Twiggy wanders off, mumbling under her breath and gesticulating randomly.

I take a step, but before I utter a word Twiggy calls out, "I'll get your dad's old case files. I used to have a little thing with the records tech, and I think he's still got the hots for me."

"Thanks," I shout. As the elaborate front door bangs shut, I chuckle and try to reconcile two things: 1. Someone has the "hots" for Twiggy; and

2. That someone is a "he." I mean, you get what I'm saying, right? No judgment. I just thought she was playing softball for the other team.

I wander through the stacks as I review my new life in Pin Cherry Harbor. I own a bookshop that houses some insanely valuable books. I have a bank account with a seemingly substantial amount of money in it. To borrow Twiggy's phrase, I think I have "the hots" for Sheriff Erick. I can eat burgers and fries for free whenever I want, thanks to my grandmother's storied past. I'm caretaker to a dangerous and mildly psychotic wildcat. And—will wonders never cease—I'm not an orphan.

That last one hits me hard. My disappearing dad is alive and he knows I exist. He should've gotten in touch with me. He should've acted like an adult and faced up to his responsibilities, but I'll discuss that with him face to face. Grams seems pretty certain he didn't murder anyone, but what if he did? Do I want a relationship with a homicidal convict? I've managed to take care of myself without him for twenty-one years . . .

A sharp scratch at the back door interrupts my self-evaluation. I grasp the handle and pause. "Pyewacket, if you are currently holding parts of any human in your mouth I demand that you drop them this instant." That should do it. I ease the door open.

Pyewacket snakes through the crack and zips past me. He's four-legged lightning with a little tilt in his sideways gallop. Maybe he was hit by a car before Grams rescued him?

Through the cracked door, the movement by the dumpster is clearly visible. Yellow crime-scene tape blocks off the back half of the alley, and a lone investigator places found items in evidence bags.

I close the door before she sees me.

Now where's that cat? I walk toward the front of the store, but I don't see or hear anything. "Pye, oh dear sweet Pye. Where are you?" I hope the fur-demon can't detect the sarcasm in my tone.

Something hits my head. I clutch my chest, jump, and squeak in fear.

"Ree-ow." Soft but condescending.

I wait a tick for my heart rate to return to normal and then I stoop to pick up . . . "What is this?" I turn the glossy black button over in my hand. Four holes. A large debossed anchor with a rope wrapped around it marks the surface. Not mine. I walk toward the trash bin.

Before I can toss the useless button out, Pyewacket leaps to the floor and his claws snag my pant leg. I stumble and drop the fastener.

"Reeeee-ow." A warning.

I might actually detect a slight variation in the meows. Grams said I would learn to understand him. Let's test my theory. I pick up the black button and move toward the wastebasket.

THWACK!

Pye hits me hard with a right paw. He got a chunk of ankle flesh with that one. "Okay, okay. I'll keep your trash souvenir." I slip the button in my pocket and roll my eyes. What a freaky cat.

The front door opens and there's a definite surge of excitement at the prospect of my first customer.

The surge heats up a notch as Sheriff Erick saunters toward me.

"I'm sure it goes without saying, Miss Moon, but you'll have to make other arrangements for the bookshop's waste disposal until we complete our investigation."

"Couldn't you have sent my good friend Deputy Paulsen over to deliver that message?" I tilt my head and try to look enticing.

"She's . . . I sent her . . . She's on official business." He steps closer to me and reaches toward my face.

My heart thuds. Is this happening? I want it to happen, but I assumed it would take weeks or even months to get him to see me as more than a "perp." I lean into my hope.

A strange look enters his tantalizing blue eyes.

My eyelids softly lower.

"Is that gum?"

My traitorous eyelids pop open.

He picks something off my forehead and rolls it between his fingers.

My face is most assuredly a blotchy shade of unbecoming crimson.

His full lips part in a bemused chuckle. "Yep. That's some Big Red if I'm not mistaken."

You don't say. I hope he's referring to the gum and not my befuddled countenance.

"I'd ask how you got chewing gum on your forehead, but I'm not sure I want to know." He walks his sexy behind over to the cash register and tosses the ABC gum in the trash can that he obviously knows exists. Seems like everyone in this town knows more about this bookshop than me.

"Nobody knows more than me, honey."

"*Great Gatsby!*" I did not see Grams fade in, and her wicked giggle makes me wonder how much of my indignation she witnessed.

Sheriff Erick tilts his head and raises an eyebrow. "You must really like books, Moon."

I nod emphatically. "Mmhmm." On the plus side, he's dropped the honorific, "Miss."

"I'll leave you to it then." He turns.

My gaze uncontrollably drops. He makes polyester—

He looks back.

Busted. I glance up and swallow.

Grams giggles into her ring-ensconced hand.

"I'll let you know when we've finished in the alley."

I nod and smile.

He leaves.

I exhale.

Grams whispers, "You've got it bad, dear. And I should know."

Ignoring the jab, I launch into an apology. "I'm so sorry about Cal, Grams. I didn't mean to drop that bomb on you. I thought you already knew. I thought you were back to tell me who killed him or something."

She presses her hand to her heart and takes a deep breath. "Cal was a wonderful man and a well-meaning father. I'm sorry you didn't get to meet him."

"Do you know what happened?"

"Near as I can tell, that's not how things work in between. I seem to be tethered to the bookshop, and I think you and Pye are the only one's who can see me."

"Pyewacket can see ghosts?" That cat is too much.

"He can sense me. Let's test out the visual angle."

Grams drifts toward the sleeping Pyewacket

and floats up to the top of the bookcase where the hellcat naps. She brushes her fingers through his whiskers below the scars bisecting his left eyebrow.

Pye instantly leaps into arched, Halloween-cat pose.

"It's only me, sweet kitty." Grams rubs her hand through the air along Pye's curved spine.

He moves the black tufts on his ears and flicks his short club of a tail. His large golden eyes search the air.

"I'd say 'sense' but not 'see.' Would you agree, Mitzy?"

"Agreed." I plop onto an over-stuffed ottoman at the end of a thick oak bookcase. "Grams?"

"Yes, dear."

"I'm going to look into dad's case. If you think he's innocent—"

"Now, don't misrepresent me. I never said he was innocent. I said I don't think he committed the murder. But I think you best focus your efforts on proving your own innocence before you worry about Jacob's misdeeds."

"You can't seriously think that Erick believes I killed Cal? Can you?"

"Oh, it's Erick is it?" Grams wiggles her shoulders and flashes her eyebrows up and down suggestively.

"Be serious, Grams."

"All right. Being accused of murder is serious, dear. Look what happened to your father. Cal was an important man in these parts, and Sheriff Harper will be under a lot of pressure to wrap this case up real quick and tidy. Everyone gives him a long leash because he's a war hero, but he'll have to charge someone—soon. Suspicion in a small town goes a long ways."

That can't be a thing. There's no way I'm going to jail for murder just because my dad—

"It absolutely is a 'thing.' And I suggest we put our heads together and see if we can't crack this thing before Sheriff Erick knows what hit him." Grams rubs her palms together eagerly.

"All I know is that I definitely did not kill Cal. Other than that I don't know where to start. I've never solved a murder, you know." I cross my arms and sigh.

"We've all seen an episode or two of *Murder She Wrote*, haven't we?" says Grams, encouragingly.

Oh, if we're counting television shows and movies as experience then I'm pretty sure I have a doctorate in criminology.

"That's the spirit!"

I jump. "It still freaks me out a little that you can hear my thoughts. So, new rule: If I don't say it out loud you don't get to respond. Got it?"

"I'll do my best, dear. But you have to understand it's rather all muddled together." She puts a hand to her mouth and squints her eyes. "I'll try to watch and see if your lips are moving. If your lips are moving then it's fair game."

"Fair enough." I shrug. "So where do we start?"

"You should have a notepad. Detectives always write notes."

I wiggle my smartphone. "I forgot to pay my bill, so I don't have any service. The notepad app still works, though."

"I like improvisation, Mitzy."

"What am I writing?"

"Let's make a list of all the suspects and then you can go question them!"

Boy, she's one gung-ho ghost!

"I'm just—"

"Lips didn't move, Grams. Lips did not move." I wag my finger and she covers her mouth with her hand. "Besides, people aren't going to let me question them. I'm a civilian. I can't force them to talk to me."

"Sweetheart, haven't you heard the saying 'You get more flies with honey'? You don't have to make anyone do anything. You're simply a grieving granddaughter who wants to learn as much as she can about her dearly departed grandfather." Grams' eyes twinkle.

"Oh, you're a sneaky Gram Gram."

Our raucous laughter disturbs the reclining Pyewacket.

My heart feels fuller than it has in ten years.

CHAPTER 10

THE FRONT DOOR of the bookshop bangs open. Grams vanishes.

A shout dissolves into the books. "A little help?"

Sounds like the honey-voiced Twiggy has returned. "On my way."

Twiggy balances a box on her right hip and juts her thumb toward the rusty white International parked with one tire up on the curb. "The rest are in there."

"I hope you didn't have to do anything unsavory." I chuckle.

"As a matter of fact, I have to go to bingo next Tuesday night. But I told him I'd bring a friend for his friend, so that makes us even."

I stop with a box half out of the SUV. "Am I the friend you're bringing?"

"The one and only." Twiggy pulls her foot off the huge door and it slams shut before I can get there. Great. I'm in town one day and some bingo-hall mafiosa is already pimping me out.

Three trips later, we have all the boxes inside.

"I'm not so sure about bingo, but thanks for getting these files, Twiggy. We should take them up to the apartment. I don't want anyone to find out I'm looking into my dad's case."

Twiggy nods in agreement and walks into the back room.

I guess when I said "we" she heard "not Twiggy." I unhook the chain across the stairs in protest and make five trips up and down the circular staircase. Despite the irritation with my employee, I can't help but grin when I tilt the candle and watch the secret door open into MY apartment. The glorious smell of books is less within the private rooms, but there's still the lovely feeling of being wrapped inside the pages of adventures.

I line all the boxes up and rest my hands on my hips. I'll need thumbtacks and string. I've watched *Elementary*. I know I'm going to need a visual representation of the connections between the suspects in the case. I'm not an idiot.

I run down the stairs—and trip over the blasted chain, which the helpful Twiggy has resecured.

Is that a muffled chuckle? Do I hear a chuckle? I

jump up and storm into the back room. "Did you hook the chain?"

"Did you unhook it?"

Is this a Mexican standoff? Actually, no. If my movie knowledge serves me, a Mexican standoff requires three people—one of whom must be Salma Hayek. I choose not to take the bait. "I need thumbtacks and string, or possibly yarn."

"You got it, boss." Twiggy rolls her chair back to the desk and continues typing information into the computer.

"Do we have any?"

"Any what?" Clickety-clack go the keys.

"Tacks and string?"

"I put 'em on the weekly order."

I don't believe her, but even if I did . . . "I need them today. Actually now would be great."

"Rex's." She does not stop typing.

It's like she's speaking in a code and I don't have the decoder ring. "Excuse me?"

"If you can't wait for the order, you'll have to toddle on down to Rex's and see if she's got what you want."

"Rex is a she?"

Twiggy slowly turns her chair like a villain in a Bond film. "What is it with you?"

I shrug and gesture for her to answer my query.

"Rex was a man. A man that owned a five and

dime in Pin Cherry Harbor. When that man up and died of natural causes seven and a half years ago, his wife took over the store. She runs Rex's Drugstore located at 414 Main Street." She rotates back to the screen, shaking her head in bewilderment.

I'm not proud to admit that I make an inappropriate gesture to the back of her smug little grey head before I leave.

Grams gives a "tsk, tsk" at me as I walk out. "Lips didn't move," I growl through my clenched teeth.

The crisp early-evening air on Main Street blows my frustration away and I take a deep cleansing breath. Not like a crystal-crunching, aura-scrubbing cleansing breath—just a nice deep breath of fresh air.

My stomach growls when I pass Myrtle's Diner. Tacks and string can wait. Mama needs some fries. I push open the door. Once again, all eyes turn.

"Hey, Mitzy. Have a seat. I'll throw your burger down."

I nod and smile. Seriously, a huge self-satisfied, face-splitting grin. I'm a regular. "Thanks, Odell."

"Cheese?"

"I'm feeling Swiss."

"I've got American."

Oh Icarus, you flew too high. "American will be divine."

Divine? Did I just refer to cheese as divine? I glance around the diner and don't see any faces I recognize. Good, no witnesses.

The rasp of polyester against vinyl precedes the appearance of a short, squat figure sliding out of a booth. Spoke too soon.

"Glad to see you haven't tried to make a run for it." Deputy Paulsen rests one hand on her pistol. "I've got my eye on you. Stay close." She wipes the grease from the corner of her mouth with the back of her hand.

"Geez," I mumble, as the front door swings shut.

"Ah, don't mind Pauly. She's had a bee in her bonnet ever since Sheriff Harper won the election, again."

Oooh, small town gossip!

"They still lookin' at you for Cal's murder?"

Oooh, small town gossip. See what I did there?

"Erick says he's waiting for time of death from the medical examiner, but Silas took a copy of my bus ticket down to the station, so I expect to be cleared soon."

I'm aware of the looks and murmurs from the four-top in the corner, but apparently this is how things are done in a small town. "So, the deputy's name is Polly Paulsen?"

"Yep, but on account of her dad wantin' a boy so bad he spelled it like the apostle Paul, and then threw the 'y' on there to give it a girlie flair."

"So it's Pauly Paulsen? I'd change my name."

Odell catches my eye through the orders-up window and a mischievous grin spreads across his face. "That right, Mizithra?"

Sic burn, old man. Sic burn. I shake my head and Odell delivers my food. "No server on the night shift?"

"If you mean a waitress, I manage all right most nights. Tally's daughter comes in on weekends for the rush."

I glance around at the sprinkling of patrons. "Mmhmm."

As I devour the burger, I have to admit that the hot, melty cheese actually is divine. I finish off the perfectly golden fries and lean back.

"Made short work of that." Odell tosses his observation across the diner without judgment.

"What can I say? I worked up an appetite today." I grab my dishes and slide them into the bin under the counter. Call it instinct or years of food-service employment. There's always a bin under the counter.

"Thanks, Mitzy."

"My compliments to the chef."

I walk out and make a hard right toward Rex's. The self-satisfied smile evaporates when the door does not budge under my efforts.

"They close at four, dear."

A woman who bears a striking resemblance to Tally, but with a backcombed monstrosity of grey hair rather than a tightly wrapped bun of flaming red, taps her watch as she walks past.

"Tilly?" I blurt.

She stops and spins on her pink kitten heels. "Do I know you, dear?"

I extend my hand as I say, "I'm Mitzy Moon. Isadora's granddaughter. I inherited the bookshop." That last one turns the lights on.

"Oh, of course. Twiggy mentioned something about being under new management. She's such a hoot."

Is she, though? "I guess that makes me the new management," I reply with a friendly wink.

"Come on by tomorrow and we'll get you all set up with a new passbook and your own box of checks."

Oh, how extravagant. I wonder what checks do? "Well, thank you kindly, Tilly—Tally—Tilly." I blush profusely. "Sorry about that. I'll see you to-morrow, Tilly."

The click-scrape of her kitten heels on the uneven cement sidewalk fades as she turns the corner.

A cold, late-summer wind blows down Main Street, pulling the damp chill from the massive body of water and spreading it over the town. I hug my arms around my middle.

I'm suddenly too aware of being alone on the street. I duck my head and jog back to the bookshop.

String or no string. It's time I learn something about Jacob Duncan.

CHAPTER 11

I HOIST OPEN the massive front door and come face to face with Twiggy.

"You need me to come in tomorrow?" She turns and slides by me.

It's an undeniable fact that I could use a more thorough tour of the bookshop. However, I have no idea if I can afford a paid guide. "Do I pay you?"

"Your Grams and I had an understanding."

"I assumed. Do you want to have an understanding with me?"

She nods.

"I'm meeting with Tilly tomorrow. Once I get a handle on the bank account, I'll see what I can offer you."

"Accounts. Bank accounts," Twiggy corrects.

I swallow my retort. "Like I said, after my

meeting with Tilly." I try a new tactic. "Can I meet you at Myrtle's for lunch?" The moment of surprise on her face pleases me.

"I gotta eat." She shrugs and walks off down the street. Not the street that runs beside the shop, which is Main, but the one in front of Bell, Book & Candle, which is—

Stepping off the curb, I search for a street sign because I can't remember the address of my own bookstore. "First Avenue." Makes perfect sense. It is the first "avenue" on this end of town. There's the enormous lake, my bookshop, and this street is the first intersection on Main. Not terribly creative, but accurate.

I walk into my bookshop and twist the locks into position on the large door.

Twiggy must shut off the lights as part of her closing procedure. I fumble for my phone in the eerie, semi-dark store. The bookcases feel oppressive in the low light, and I make a mental note to hire an electrician to pull some wire and place a light switch right next to the front entrance.

I deftly step over the chain and make my way to the candle handle. I chuckle as I reach for the device.

"Oh good, you're finally back."

I make another mental note to purchase adult diapers to staunch the flow of ghost-related pants accidents I've been having. "Grams, you've got to come up with a more subtle entrance strategy."

"Sorry, dear. I started to go a little coffin-crazy once you left. Twiggy can't see or hear me, and I can't leave the bookshop. I was anxious. Maybe over anxious."

I walk into the apartment and the lights automatically switch on with a slow ramp up to full power. I place my hands on my hips. "Now why didn't you put one of these do-hickeys at the front door?"

"Doesn't make sense to have the lights flicking off and on every time someone walks in the front door!"

I shake my head and put on my onesie reindeer pajamas. "Time to reopen this old case."

Off comes the lid of file box number one.

Choking on the dust, I grab a cloth from the bathroom and wipe down all the boxes before returning to the first time capsule.

"Good idea, dear."

It's nice to have a cheering section—even for the mundane.

Grams smiles and begins a reply to my unspoken thought. "I—"

I point to my lips, which did not move, and Grams nods. We're establishing ground rules. Which seems important in any inter-species communication. Oh, and I've decided ghosts are a different species.

The first evidence box contains police reports and witness statements. I learn that the robbery took place right after closing and that Jacob and Darrin came in through an unsecured employee entrance on the loading dock.

The statements are all from employees of the box store. None contain details about the shooting. After a cursory review, I deduce that my father, Darrin, and the store manager were the only people in the room containing the safe and later the corpse.

I make a pile of witness statements. I place the security guard statement on top of that pile. He's the only one who noticed any kind of detail. The other statements were just the emotional accusations of traumatized employees.

It's unclear whether the other employees knew a robbery was in progress prior to the gunshot. Each statement seems quite fuzzy up to the point of the sound of a gun.

"Do you think he did it, dear?"

The hairs on the back of my neck stand at attention. "I forgot you were here, Grams."

"I was doing my best not to jump into your internal debate. Weren't there any security cameras in the room where the safe was?"

I pick up the police report and scan through it a

second time. "Says here that the camera was disabled by gunshot. Also says the perps took the tape and smashed the security equipment."

"Make a note on your phone thingy."

I swipe open the app and stare at Grams. "Do you think they took the tape before or after?" I type a quick note.

"If it was before, wouldn't the guard have tried to stop them?"

I make another note and move toward file box number two.

By the time I lift the lid off box number five, sunlight paints grey streaks across my ceiling. "What time is it?"

"How would I know, honey? Time has no meaning on this side."

I press a button on my phone and yawn. It's 5:13 a.m. "I better get a few hours sleep before I open the shop."

"I'll wait over here." Grams floats to a beautiful scalloped-back chair in the corner and hovers near the puffy seat.

"Can you 'fade out' or something? It's unnerving to have you floating in a corner watching me."

"Of course, dear."

I wonder if she's genuinely gone or just in "low power" mode so I can't see her. I swear there's a chuckle coming from somewhere. Oh well, too tired to care.

I flop onto the four-poster bed and snuggle into the heavenly mattress, Egyptian cotton sheets, and sumptuous down comforter.

Dreamland holds no rest for me. The robbery plays out from every angle in my nightmares. I watch my father fire the gun over and over.

When Pyewacket jumps onto the bed, compressing my chest and shocking me instantly awake, I actually feel relief. My time under the comforter hasn't delivered any rest.

I rub the sleep from my eyes and absently scratch my fingers between Pye's ears. He's suspiciously docile. Is that purring? It sounds like a small lawnmower. Choosing caution, I pull my hand back. "What are you up to, you wicked kitten?"

"He's hungry." Grams swirls closer.

"Holy Hera!" I don't think I peed this time, but a ghost greeting first thing in the morning is definitely unsettling. My heart is certainly pumping blood with all its might now. Rise and shiver, I say.

I blink, yawn, and scrape a hand through my haystack of a hairdo. "I have to feed him? I thought he was a free agent. Don't bobcats kill mice or something?"

"Pyewacket is a caracal and he can certainly take care of himself, dear. However, he needs a human to open the box of Fruity Puffs and pour them into his bowl."

"Come again?" I look at the fiendish feline and try to reconcile him munching on kids cereal. "Fruity Puffs?"

"It's his little treat. I spoiled him." Grams floats her hand along his back.

Pye responds with an unsettlingly loud purr.

"And now that spoiling falls to me, I suppose?"

"Would you?"

I chuckle and shake my head.

Downstairs in the back room I locate the cereal. Pye threads himself around my legs in an insistent, and dangerously unbalancing, figure eight. As soon as the Fruity Puffs hit the bowl he attacks. The way he powers through the sugary treats you'd think . . . you'd think he was a spoiled child.

I bend to scratch his ears.

He emits a deep, throaty growl and a needle-clad paw swipes toward my hand.

I jump back. "Easy, tiger. I'll make a note to keep my hands to myself during Fruity Puffs feeding time."

Grams giggles. "He takes it very seriously, the little cuddle bug."

That's not the term I would've used.

A sharp knock at the front of the store interrupts our tender family moment.

I shuffle toward the door and twist the locks open.

The early morning sun wraps an enticing glow around the broad shoulders of Sheriff Erick. I steady myself on the door. "Well, good morning to you." I grin lasciviously.

"Mitzy Moon, I'm here to take you in." Sheriff Harper reaches toward me with the handcuffs.

For the first time since I laid eyes on him, I step away. "Hold on a minute, Erick. Haven't we already played this game? My lawyer supplied you with the bus ticket. There's no way I was here when Cal was killed."

He drops his hand and shakes his head. He looks genuinely sorry for what he's about to say. "I called Silas before I headed over. The ME puts time of death between 1000 and 1100 hours yesterday." He shifts his weight from one foot to the other. "The bus comes through town at 0930 and yesterday it came early, 0900 hours."

"You're serious?" I put my hands on my— Oh crap! I'm still wearing my reindeer onesie. "Can I at least change?"

Sheriff Erick shakes his head. "Sorry, but I've got to take you in. If it's any consolation, you make a cute reindeer."

A healthy glow floods my cheeks.

"You'll give her a minute to make herself presentable, Sheriff Harper." Silas places a friendly but firm hand on the sheriff's arm.

I didn't even see my lawyer arrive, but I'm grateful for the chance to put on some jeans.

"Make it quick," the sheriff says.

I manage to negotiate the chain and race into the apartment. "Grams? Grams? Are you here?"

"I don't like the look of this, dear. What will you do?"

I shrug as I wiggle into my least ripped pair of skinny jeans and the only button-down shirt I own. "I'll tell Silas to send Twiggy over," I call as I rush down the stairs.

"Is there someone else in there?" Sheriff Harper's hand moves toward his holstered weapon as he peers around me.

Think fast. Think fast. "Just Pyewacket. I didn't want him to worry." I catch Silas's eye and he nods his approval.

"I'll be sure Twiggy sees to the cat," Silas adds in support of my story.

I hold out both wrists and take no pleasure as Erick clicks the handcuffs into place.

CHAPTER 12

I RUB AT the ink on my thumb. Fingerprinted. Booked. The humiliation. I lean back against the concrete wall of the holding cell and hug my knees to my chest. Is this how it felt for my dad?

I'm sure he was upset to be accused of a crime he didn't commit. But he committed part of the crime. Everyone seems to agree that he was in on the robbery. What went wrong?

With nothing but time on my hands, I close my eyes and call up the images of the witness statements. Every single witness claimed to have heard two gunshots.

Everyone except the security guard. He claimed he heard three.

The medical examiner's report stated the victim died instantly. A single gunshot.

If the first shot was the one that took out the camera then the guard must've arrived before the manager was—

Who fired the third shot? Who destroyed the security equipment and took the tape? Why didn't anyone else hear the third shot?

I scan through the police report in my mind's eye and recall no mention of a third bullet being recovered.

"Thought you might be hungry."

The sight of Odell's concerned face and the paper sack, which I pray holds a burger and fries, nearly brings tears to my eyes. "Starving. How'd you know?"

"Paulsen comes in for breakfast every morning. You'd a thought she'd found the Lindbergh baby." Odell shakes his head and worry creases his brow.

I gently tug the bag from his hand and add, "I didn't do it."

"Only a fool'd think you did." He makes to spit on the ground but thinks better of it. "I don't like the smell of this thing, you hear me?"

I nod and shove another handful of fries into my mouth.

"Odell? What are you doing in here?" Sheriff Harper sidles up to the holding cell and looks from my benefactor to me. "She's not allowed to have visitors."

"Gotta feed your prisoners, Sheriff. This ain't a gulag." Odell ignores the sheriff and grabs the bars of my cell. "Same thing for dinner?"

Mouth full, I nod emphatically.

"Odell, I'm warning you . . . " Sheriff Harper tilts his head in earnest.

Odell waves him off and walks out of the station, as though the sheriff just announced the sky is purple and he's not having it.

"Silas said he had something to take care of, but he asked me to let you know he'd be back this afternoon." Sheriff Harper gives me an uncomfortable nod and turns.

"Erick?" I use a soft tone and let my voice crack a little.

He exhales and looks over his shoulder at the cell.

"How did the ME determine time of death?"

"Miss Moon, I'll be sure to give your lawyer a copy of the report. He can pass along the details. In the meantime, I'll ask you again to refer to me as Sheriff Harper. First degree murder is no joke."

He walks out and I lick the salt off my fingers. Murder. Like father like daughter. What an unfortunate family legacy.

The sound of a key in the cell door wakes me. I look around in momentary confusion. My all-night investigation into my father's case must've caught up to me. I rub my face and work to bring my visitor into focus. "Hey, Silas."

"You have been released on $100,000 bail." He extends a hand to help me up. "I'll return you to the bookshop. Your arraignment will be held a week from tomorrow."

I take his hand and follow him mutely out of the holding cell. I can't believe this is happening to me. This over-eager sheriff in this backwater town is actually going to accuse— "Did you say $100,000?"

"I did." Silas holds the door for me as we exit to the street.

"I don't have that kind of money. Did you post my bail? I can't repay you. I mean, I don't plan—"

"Isadora's estate is more than capable of posting bail. Now, it behooves me to remind you that you mustn't leave town. But if you're anything like your grandmother, I'll assume you're all fight and no flight."

The shock of the money is sure to be distorting my face, but the truth of his assumption pushes a smile through. "I'm a fighter. If Erick isn't going to look for any other suspects, I'll just have to do it for him."

"You may require these."

Silas lays a key ring in my hand.

I rub the emblem. "I have a Mercedes?"

"Indeed. I thought you might be in need of

transport to and from the questioning of witnesses."
He smiles and gives a little wink.

"I'll have a list of suspects by supper. Can you get me their addresses?"

"Twiggy is a resourceful woman. Folks tend to experience a degree of intimidation in her presence. Take her along as you see fit." Silas opens the door of the Model T and I slide in with a fresh sense of purpose.

Looks like I'm working two cases at once. At this rate, I'll have to hang an addendum sign in the front window: "Bell, Book & Candle Bookshop and Detective Services."

CHAPTER 13

BACK AT THE BOOKSTORE, Grams is swirling mad while Pye chases something through the stacks. If it's a mouse, I don't want to know.

Twiggy walks out of the back room and, for a split second, I swear there's concern on her face. Whatever it was is quickly replaced with cool indifference.

"Oh, you're back."

"Apparently."

"Silas give you the keys?"

"He did."

She nods and walks away.

Grams impatiently announces, "I have two names for that list, dear. Start writing or tapping. There's no time to lose."

Once I retreat to the safety of the apartment, I

whip out my phone and prepare to take dictation. "Whenever you're ready, Grams."

"Top of the list has to be Cal's gold-digging third wife, Kitty Zimmerman-Duncan. And write down her boyfriend, too."

I pause and raise an eyebrow. "She has a boyfriend?"

"She's thirty years younger than Cal, pumped full of collagen, Botox, and a set of—"

"Grams!"

"What can I say? I never liked her. Too fake. From her misappropriated British colloquialisms to her Jessica Rabbit hair . . . I thought Cal could do better."

Not my place to say, but it sounds like my Grams may be more than a little jealous.

"Well, it's—"

I point to my lips.

Grams crosses her arms and swirls angrily around the apartment.

"I've written 'The trollop's boyfriend' on the list, if that makes you feel better."

"Thank you. It does."

I chew the inside of my cheek. "That's not a very long list."

"Truth is, dear, Cal and I drifted apart these past few years. I don't know who he was doing business with or which folks were in his new social circle." Grams places a hand over her heart and sighs.

"That's all right. I'll see if I can meet with Kitty and maybe she'll let something useful slip."

"Yes. One day at a time. That's all any of us can manage."

I get a strong AA vibe from that comment, but I let it lie. Too late. I try to stuff the thought down, but I catch Grams looking at me with a pained expression. The kind of regret I've had on many a morning after. I smile and nod.

She does the same.

It's probably best if I change the subject. "Silas mentioned that I might take Twiggy along on the interrogations."

"Oh, not on this one, honey. Kitty has a golden stick so far up her—"

"Grams!"

She giggles uncontrollably. "I guess my roots are showing."

"Do you come from a long line of street fighters?" I chuckle.

"As a matter of fact, I played a little roller derby before I met Odell. There were actually a few contenders before Odell—truth be told." A mischievous grin plays across her ghostly lips.

"The truth will have to be told at a later date, Grams. Where can I find Kitty?"

She looks down her nose at me and scrunches her face like there's a bad smell in the air. "You won't get within fifty yards of her looking like something Pye dragged in."

I walk toward my duffle.

"Unless you're hiding the Queer Eye guys in that bag, dear, you're going to need to borrow something from my closet."

I can't picture myself wearing some sixty-five-year-old lady's clothes. I roll my eyes.

Grams swirls toward the closet. "Oh, ye of little faith."

I open the door and the lights pop on with flair. My jaw drops. "Holy crap, Grams!"

She chuckles with satisfaction as I step into a closet right out of *Sex and the City* meets *Confessions of a Shopaholic.*

Just to be clear, I love clothes. The fact that I wear ripped skinny jeans and snarky T-shirts is my protest to poverty, not a fashion choice. I walk reverently through the closet and my fingers dance across the fabrics. Yes, I said fabrics. I'm on Project Runway now.

"You'll want the aquamarine tea-length dress with the Valentino T-straps. Kitty's got a thing for Valentinos."

I pull the padded hanger supporting the lovely

frock and check the tag. "Matthew Christopher? Must've been one special occasion."

"I married Cal in that dress."

I turn and see little apparition tears rolling down Grams' cheeks.

"I can't possibly wear this, Grams."

"I want you to, dear. I'll never get to wear it again . . . He always said I looked like an angel fallen from heaven in it."

I hold the dress in front of me and gaze into the full-length mirror. "Oh brother. I better start with a shower."

Grams chuckles. "And they say wisdom is wasted on the young."

I won't bore you with the particulars, but let's agree that it is the single most enjoyable, all-hot-water-no-surprises shower of my life.

I sit down at the marble-topped vanity and stare at my freshly scrubbed reflection. I get a flash of my mother's face and I smile wistfully. Memories of sitting on the Formica counter in the bathroom of our studio apartment watching her "put on her face" drift softly into my consciousness. She would explain each step to me as though she were a warrior preparing for battle.

"This is called foundation and it covers up any weak spots or imperfections so I look ready to conquer the world."

I miss the sound of her voice.

"The blush gives me a little color so they can't tell I'm running on four hours' sleep."

I remember she worked at least two jobs, but maybe it was three. Time erases so much.

"This cinnamon mocha lip tint gives me a confident smile, but keeps it professional."

Her smile could lift the clouds from any bad day.

"A gentle application of smoky shadow gives my eyes depth and intelligence. Not that I'm not intelligent, this just confirms their suspicions."

I know that my smarts absolutely came from her.

"Always give the eyebrows a light nudge with a pencil, so you look like you mean business."

Then she would apply a little mascara to my lashes before she coated her own and finish by saying, "Dark lashes give you a finished look. Serious but mysterious." And she would kiss the tip of my nose, every single morning until—

I twist the mascara wand back into the tube and blink back the tears that are threatening to fall.

"I would've loved your mother, Mitzy."

A wave of self-conscious heat flushes my skin. I whip the towel off my head and fluff my white-blonde locks. "What am I going to do with this?"

Grams swirls around and chews on her thumbnail. "This will be tricky, since I can't physically move anything around. But if you can follow instructions, I'm sure we can brush you into debutante status in no time."

"I'm game for anything."

Ghost cosmetology school is in session.

I've never spent this much time on my hair in my life. Prior to the "Bad Bet" haircut after my karaoke humiliation, I was a high-pony or messy-bun girl every day.

The application of "product" and the judicious use of a blow dryer and styling wand create a sleek, socialite look. "I'm a knockout, Grams."

"Give me a little credit, dear. I did have five husbands and an undisclosed number of 'special friends.'"

"Grams! I'm shocked by what I'm hearing."

"Don't get all high and mighty with me, Mitzy. You talk in your sleep, and this Shady Ben you mumble about sounds like he was a *very* special friend."

"Ouch." Who knew ghosts could be so nosy and merciless.

"All right, off you go."

"Where exactly am I going?"

Grams freeze-frames for a split second before answering. "I think I heard you say it's Thursday. Is it the first Thursday of the month?"

I take a quick look at my phone. "Yup."

"Oh, she'll be at the mansion hosting the Duncan Club monthly luncheon."

"Maybe I should go another time." I tug at the gorgeous dress and wiggle my toes in the Valentinos.

"Nonsense. We didn't get you all gussied up for nothin'. You get in that fancy Mercedes and you walk into that luncheon like you own the place. After all, your pedigree is far better than hers. You're a Duncan by blood, dear."

Ooooh, I have a pedigree.

CHAPTER 14

As I DRIVE out to the mansion, I can't help but think about how much I *don't* miss my old life. My pattern of over-socializing and drinking to dull the pain of my disappointments and loneliness wasn't as fulfilling as I thought. I haven't had a drink since I arrived in this tiny town in almost-Canada, and I've been too busy to miss anything. My short flash of personal reflection is interrupted when I spy my landmark ahead on the right.

A large granite stone bears what I can only assume is the Duncan family crest with a large "D" in the center. I turn, pass through the massive wrought-iron gates, and continue down the drive. And it is a drive, not a driveway. I can't even see the house as I curve gently through the thick birch trees. The blur of black-and-white peeling bark is a little mesmerizing.

It's impossible to resist playing a moment of what-if as I fantasize about growing up this wealthy.

The drive straightens and I am struck by the sheer size of the mansion. It sits on the shore of the great lake that graces the entire region with its presence, but this massive home actually rivals the body of water.

It's easy to see my younger self running through the trees and skipping stones across the lake.

The slate slabs of the driveway curve widely to the left, allowing room for fifteen to twenty cars to park in front of the three divided two-car garages. Two soaring gables sit astride a magnificent entrance, and light spills through massive windows. The entire home is faced in split rock, and at least three chimneys poke through the steeply sloped roof. A terraced patio hugs the side of the home and works its way toward the surging waves.

My daydream evaporates like mist over the water. I need to focus and get my game face on.

I drive past the fifteen cars lining the drive. I park the Mercedes, pop the door, and step out.

Before I walk into who knows what kind of society luncheon, I take a minute to admire my wheels. A 1957 silver Mercedes 300SL coupe with those sexy, gullwing doors. I whistle softly under my breath, slip the key into my vintage beaded handbag, and swallow. "Game on, Moon."

My heels click magnificently against the stone, and the deep resonant gong of the doorbell does not disappoint. I'm not surprised when an aptly dressed maid opens the massive wooden double-doors.

"May I help you?" Her eyes take in my attire and find it acceptable.

"I certainly hope so. I'm looking for Kitty." I thought about using the "Mrs. Zimmerman-Duncan" option, but I thought "Kitty" might make it seem more like we were loosely acquainted.

"The ladies' club meets in the Fireplace Room." She turns and walks soundlessly across the hardwood floor.

I follow, painfully aware of the clunking of my heels.

She stops, gives a little bow, and gestures me into the space.

I almost ask her to point out Kitty. No need. If Jessica Rabbit came to life and traded her sultry voice for a cheap, imitation faux British accent . . . I give you, Kitty Zimmerman-Duncan.

I choose to "mix" a bit before I introduce myself to the hostess. Maybe I'll overhear something useful.

"I'm gutted, I tell you, gutted. He was my

world." Kitty dabs a finger under her unwet eye while several orbiters murmur their concern.

"Have they found the killer?" A short brunette, who is clearly playing out of her league, asks the indelicate question.

"They arrested someone straightaway, which was brilliant, but Pauly told me the woman is already out on bail."

So Deputy Paulsen has a direct line to Kitty. Good to know.

"Do you need any help with the arrangements, love?"

This older woman looks to have quite a pedigree, and I take note of the massive yellow diamond on her left hand.

"Oh, Chantelle, I super love that you would make such an offer. That's just brilliant. I think I have everything sorted. Thank you so much." Kitty's hand presses against her double-Ds, and her face struggles to make an expression. I'm guessing the Botox interferes.

As I'm about to make another pass through the gaggle—it happens.

"Do I see a new face? Oh, the Duncan Club adores new members. How brills!"

I'm caught like a deer in headlights. I fumble with a smile and debate whether a curtsy is required.

She extends a shockingly pedicured hand weighed down by several carats of blue diamonds. "I'm Kitty Zimmerman-Duncan. Welcome to my humble home."

I hope she doesn't see me gag as I take the bejeweled limb and delicately shake. I don't know what possesses me but for some reason I say, "Mizithra Moon, darling. So good to meet."

The name has the desired effect.

Her eyes widen and she takes in my attire, all the way down to the Valentinos.

"Are those? Oh they are! Oh brilliant!" She pulls me into her inner circle and whispers, "I've never met a pair of Valentinos I didn't love. I'd kill for those." I believe that eye twitch was meant to be a wink, but again, the Botox must prevent many of her simple facial functions.

"Is there somewhere we can chat in private?" I whisper and give an actual wink.

She ushers me up three separate sets of stairs, two steps each, and through some curved glass doors.

This showy wine cellar is bigger than my old apartment. Geez! I swallow the disgust and return to the mission at hand.

"What is it, love? If the dues are a bit too much to pay in one go, I'm happy to let it slide for a month or two. Our little secret." She pats my hand and steals another glance at my shoes.

"Actually, it's about Cal." Wait for it . . .

She presses the diamond-weighted hand to the double-Ds and gasps. "Oh, the pain is still so fresh."

I'm not getting any sincerity from that, but it could be the lack of emotion on her plastic face. I break my news. "He was my grandfather, and I'm so upset that I didn't get a chance to meet him." I hope my pained expression carries more authenticity.

She steps back and narrows her gaze. "Are you — Are you Jacob's kid?"

Now that was decidedly un-British. I detect a hint of angry New Yorker. I place a hand over my mouth and nod.

To her credit, she recovers rapidly. "Oh you poor dear. I'll ask Svenka to make you some tea. Chantelle can run the meeting. We'll slip up to the study and the two of us can have a dash of girl chat. What do you say?"

"That would be divine." What is it lately with me and that word? Granted, a chat is more divine than cheese, but get a grip, Mitzy.

Kitty slips out of the wine cellar and signals to the maid. They exchange hushed words.

A strange shiver ripples across my skin. Is this the scene in a James Bond film where two enormous goons walk in, drag me off screen, and then we cut to them tying me to a platform above a shark tank?

The maid, Svenka, leans to the right and sizes me up with an overly plucked raised eyebrow before scurrying off to do her mistress's bidding.

Looks like I'll be spared the unnecessarily complicated death scene, this time.

Kitty returns, all smiles, and escorts me up to the study—coffered ceiling and all. She takes a seat on one of the curvaceous leather chaises and gestures for me to take the other.

I admire the drama of the piece, but I don't know how to sit on it. I'm sure it would provide a fabulous place to lie back and nap, but it's tricky to find a lady-like purchase on the undulating surface. I opt for a prim perch on the edge of the large curve and smile at Kitty.

"When did you arrive in Pin Cherry, Mizithra?"

I almost correct her, but luckily I remember that I chose the proper version of my name to accompany my ridiculous hairdo and frock. "Unfortunately, I arrived too late." I'm the one running this interrogation. I can't let her take over. "How long had you known my grandfather?"

"Oh, we first met almost fifteen years ago in Aspen. Cal loved to ski."

"Did you live in Colorado?" If I were a gold-digger, I would guess the slopes of a high-end Aspen ski resort would be prime real estate.

"I lived there seasonally."

Translation, she worked for the ski resort or for some local establishment. "Oh, how fun. Was it love at first sight?"

She hesitated before pasting on a huge, wrinkle-free smile. "I can't speak for Cal, but I thought he was brilliant fun the moment I met him."

"How sweet." I swallow my nausea. "Did he propose right away?"

She twists her huge diamond ring and shifts her position on the chaise. "He wanted me to meet his friends, and— Anyway, I came back to Pin Cherry Harbor with him and we were engaged that spring."

"Did you start the Duncan Club?"

She stiffens and eyes me suspiciously. "Not that you would know, but his second wife, Isadora, started the Club."

"Oh, I didn't know." Grams failed to mention that nugget. "What does the Club do?"

"Well, I'm not sure what Isadora had planned, but when I took over I wanted the Club to provide exclusive social opportunities to Pin Cherry's deserving women."

By deserving, I assume she means the wealthy

and the social climbers. "Do you have events other than the luncheons?"

Her whole face lights up. "Oh yes. We have three fundraisers each year. The Halloween Masquerade was Cal's favorite. It was always the most successful. We held it at the old Wells Iron Ore Refinery. The huge building was the perfect place for a haunted ball."

"Sounds wonderful. I wish I could've seen it." I almost convince myself of my interest with that line.

"Oh, you'll have to come this year—if you're still in town. It'll be brilliant." She pats her hands together eagerly. "Cal would've wanted it to continue."

I'm not sure if she's trying to convince herself or me. "When was the last time you saw my grandfather?"

"Monday morning, I suppose." She brushes the pleat of her skirt and smiles.

"I thought he died on Wednesday? You didn't see him on Tuesday or Wednesday?"

She stands and paces to the study's large bay window. "The stress of the trauma is making me lose track of time. I guess Wednesday at breakfast would've been our last moment together." She presses hand to ample chest. "I'm sorry. I still get so emotional."

I bustle over and pat her shoulder. "I'm so sorry to put you through all this. I'll leave you to your grief, Kitty. I didn't mean to stir up the pain."

She nods and bites her collagen-stuffed lip.

"I'll see myself out."

She turns as I leave and says, "Thank you for your understanding, Mizithra. So many people have misjudged my relationship with Cal. I loved him for so much more than his money."

Her words, not mine. "Of course you did, dear." I nod and smile.

CHAPTER 15

GRAMS IS FIT to be tied by the time I return to the shop.

"What's gotten into you?" I ask.

"I never thought I would be treated more unfairly in death than in life!" She swirls up to the high ceiling and floats down in a slow spiral of self-pity.

I look around the massive bookshop and spin the Mercedes keys around my finger. I'm having a tiny bit of trouble seeing where life treated her poorly. "I'm not sure I understand."

"They won't tell me anything about Cal. I'm his wife! I should have rights, dear. Even if this is the afterlife, I should still have rights." More swirling.

It may be the wrong time to point out that she

was not technically his wife when he died. Instead I change the subject. "You were spot on about Kitty."

If a ghost can change from out of order to Vegas neon in the blink of an eye, that's how I would describe the switch that flipped in Grams. "Tell me everything," she purrs.

I relay the sequence of events as best I can, despite the incessant interruptions.

"Good call using Mizithra, dear. Anything that sounds even remotely hoity-toity blows that girl's skirt up."

"Do you think it's odd that she's planning to hold the Halloween Masquerade without Cal?"

"Why is that odd?" Grams shrugs.

"Kitty, said it was always Cal's favorite. I thought maybe it would be rude to have it without him."

"Halloween, Cal's favorite? That doesn't sound right. That man hated costumes of any kind. He wouldn't even wear matching sweaters for the family Christmas photos."

I whip out my phone and make a note of that. "There was one other thing . . . " My voice drifts off as I type up my concern.

"And?" Grams hovers anxiously.

"Oh, I didn't realize I stopped talking." I put the phone down. "She said the last time she saw Cal was Monday morning. When I mentioned he was killed on Wednesday, she claimed PTSD and said she must've had breakfast with him on Wednesday."

Grams darkens. "Where was he for two days?"

"Maybe nowhere, Grams. Maybe Kitty was confused and she did see him Wednesday. I just thought it was worth mentioning."

She gestures to the phone. "You made a note?"

I nod.

"Good. Who's our next suspect?"

"The only thing she mentioned was some iron ore refinery. Do you know who owns that old place?"

"It used to belong to the Wells family, but I heard the bank foreclosed on it . . . " Grams drifts toward the floor. "Tilly would know."

Tilly! "Oh crap! I was supposed to meet with Tilly today—and meet Twiggy for lunch." I turn and run out the front door and down Main Street.

I grab the door of Myrtle's Diner and pause to catch my breath. I pull the door open, spy Twiggy, and blurt my breathless apology. "So . . . sorry."

A whistle from the kitchen grabs my attention.

"Who do we have here?" says Odell with a chuckle.

"No idea," adds Twiggy. "I hope you have some filet mignon back there, Odell."

I look down at my designer gown and shoes.

Crap. "All right, get it out of your system." I walk to the table and take a seat in the booth opposite the cackling Twiggy. "I'll have my usual, Odell."

"Right away, M'lady." He barely completes the gibe before his guffaws join the fray.

I take a deep breath and raise my finger to let them both have a taste of my fancy rage—

"Miss Moon?" Sheriff Harper stands in the middle of the diner, looking like he's just seen a ghost.

Ah, what the hell. I stand and place one hand at my boned-and-stayed waist. "Erick."

"You look . . . That's a real—" He swallows several times and looks around the near-empty diner as the color creeps across his cheeks. "Were you out at the Duncan place this morning?"

"I was." Clearly he already knows the answer to this pop quiz. I have the urge to reach over and muss his hair. I love it when those long bangs hang—

"I'll have to ask you to stay clear of this case, Miss Moon." He squares his shoulders.

My heart flutters. "Your *case*, is it? Does that mean you might actually be looking at someone besides me as a suspect in my grandfather's murder?"

"I'm not at liberty to discuss the case, Miss Moon."

I decide to press my advantage. I swish closer to the sheriff. Close enough for the layers of my tulle skirt to brush against his polyester pants. It looks sexier than it sounds. "We both know I didn't kill him, Erick. Why don't you share your news with me and I'll share mine."

He carefully scoots back and his boots squeak against the flooring. "What news?"

"My step-gramma was feeling chatty this morning." I smile in what I hope looks like a cat-that-got-the-canary kind of grin.

He shakes his head in defeat. "It'll be in the official report soon enough. The ME recanted the initial time of death."

I lean toward the lovely specimen of manhood. "Go on."

"I'm afraid I can't say any more. The new time of death could be critical to uncovering additional suspects."

I can't seem to stop myself from putting a hand on his arm. Goodness, that bicep is exactly as firm as I imagined.

"Excuse me, Miss Moon." He flushes pure magenta and tugs his arm.

I tighten my grasp. "Would it interest you to know that Kitty said the last time she saw Cal was Monday morning?"

His eyes widen and his pupils dilate. I hope I'm

the reason for the dilation, but my celebration is short lived.

He pulls free and hustles out of the diner before I can say another word.

Twiggy gives me a slow clap. "Looks like you've got 'em on the run."

I turn back to the booth and look around in confusion. Gosh darn it, that man makes me lose all sense of time.

"Your burger's comin' out in a minute, Mitzy. You want a bib or something?"

I toy with a witty comeback, but when I remember the pride in Isadora's eyes as I slipped into this piece of her history, I choose propriety. "Yes, maybe a couple."

Covered in clean dishtowels and fortified with fries, I remember why I'm meeting Twiggy. "I didn't get a chance to stop by the bank." I gesture to my getup.

"I figured," she responds.

"I'll be heading over there after lunch and then I can meet you at the bookshop to discuss your pay." I shove the last fry in my mouth and lick the salt off my fingers.

Twiggy looks me up and down. "Talk about making a silk purse out of a sow's ear."

I stop with my pinky finger half in half out of my mouth. What can I say? She's right. I shrug.

"Before you turn yourself inside out"—Twiggy slides out of the booth—"your Grams never paid me. We were best friends." She walks past me and calls back. "You and I—we're good."

The door swishes open and closed. I look at Odell and he salutes me with his metal spatula. "That's a tough nut to crack, that one. Good for you."

I'm not sure what I did to earn Twiggy's loyalty, but I'm in no position to refuse allies. I thank Odell for the delicious food and stroll over to the bank.

I bask in the effect of my luscious outfit on the public at large.

Tilly rushes to my side when I enter the bank. "Good afternoon. How can I help you, Miss."

"Hi, Tilly. You told me to stop by to get something called 'checks.'" I smile broadly.

She's obviously taken aback. "Miss Moon? Oh my stars, I didn't recognize you in that—" She stops herself and blinks rapidly. "Well, don't you just look divine?"

Looks like I'm not the only one who defaults to that word under pressure.

She walks back to her meager brown desk and beckons me to follow.

I press my advantage while she's discombobulated. "Tilly, are you familiar with the Wells Iron Ore Refinery?"

"Of course. They were the largest employer in the region during the boom years." She doesn't look up from her paper shuffling but takes a form and loads it into a typewriter.

I lose my train of thought as I stare in fascination at the device I have only read about in old books.

"Why do you ask?"

Oh, right. I'm supposed to be gathering information. "When did the refinery go into receivership?" I hope that's the right word . . .

"Receivership?"

Crap. Wrong word.

"Oh, no dear. The bank doesn't own that property. Finnegan settled the loan almost two years ago." She cranks the little knob and feeds the form through the typewriter.

"Finnegan?"

"Yes, Finnegan Wells. He's the great-grandson and current owner."

"But I thought the refinery was abandoned. How could he afford to pay off the debt if the iron ore business dried up?"

Tilly looks up from her forms. "I'm sure I have no idea, dear. What's your sudden interest in iron ore?"

Oops. Pushed too hard. "No interest. Just making conversation."

She pinches her lips together and raises an eyebrow.

"Do you need me to sign anything? Oh, Twiggy mentioned that there's more than one account. Do you have statements for me?"

She gets up without a word and returns with two thick files. "We keep the records in the vault. I'll have the clerk make copies for you."

"You don't have electronic records?"

"How's that, dear?"

I slowly scan across the tidy wooden desks in the bank. I don't see any computers. What if I slipped through some kind of time portal when I stepped off that bus? Maybe I did fall into an old black-and-white movie. No computers? I open my vintage handbag in a panic. I touch my smartphone and breathe a sigh of relief. Okay, technology does exist—just not in this bank. "How do you keep track of deposits and withdrawals?"

Tilly looks at me as though I have a tentacle growing out of my neck. "That's what the passbook is for, Miss Moon." She slides three small books the size of passports across the desk and lays a form in front of me. "Sign at the bottom. Press firmly. You have to get through three copies."

I sign the top page and lift it up to sign the next page. There on the yellow sheet my signature already exists. "What is this?" I lift the yellow sheet and my signature already exists on the pink sheet, too. "How did—?"

Tilly looks at me for a moment. "It's called NCR paper. The carbon is built into each sheet so the signature transfers through. That's why I told you to press firmly." She smiles and shakes her head in amusement.

I stare at the paper as though it possesses magical powers.

"You get the pink copy. The white copy goes in your permanent file, and the yellow copy stays at the teller window in case you need to make a withdrawal and forget your passbook."

I don't have a clue what any of those words mean. I take the pink sheet and the three little books and walk out of the time machine in a daze.

CHAPTER 16

The Bell, Book & Candle is as "not busy" as usual when I return. Twiggy carefully shelves books and Pyewacket is nowhere to be found.

"Grams? Grams?"

"Don't look at me," volunteers Twiggy. "I can't see her."

I negotiate the chain in my heels and teeter up the stairs to the apartment. I drop the paperwork on the bed and unbuckle the tiny T-straps on the Valentinos. As my feet sink into the thick area rug I let out a sigh.

"Don't complain, honey. I know ten women who would kill to wear those shoes for five minutes."

"Grams!" I smile and rub my poor tootsies. "Trust me, if I'd only had to wear them for five minutes I wouldn't be complaining." I wiggle out of the dress and eagerly slip back into skinny jeans and a snarky tee. However, when I look in the mirror I have to admit that I miss the knockout a little.

Grams shoots ahead of me into the closet. "You can't hang that up in here, Mitzy."

I look at the dress and then at Grams. "I'm not sure what you're saying. Where am I meant to hang it?"

"Darling, you wore it for hours. You have to take it and have it properly cleaned."

"Like a dry cleaners?" Girls with skinny jean and T-shirt wardrobes don't get much dry-cleaner action.

"Exactly. Take it down to Harbor Cleaners on 3rd Avenue. Tanya knows how I like it."

"Now?"

"Now."

Copy that, as they say in the film business. I slip on my kicks and march down the street to see Tanya about my fancy ghost gramma's couture cleaning needs. There's a sentence I never expected to utter in my life.

Shockingly, there's a man in line in front of me at the cleaners. It's the first time I've had to wait for anything in Pin Cherry and the experience intrigues. He's mid forties, fit for his age, with a surprising amount of thick black hair. I imagine he's a hot property in these parts.

A woman returns from the back. That must be Tanya. Her movement stirs the atmosphere and a fresh wave of chemically impregnated air wafts over me. Ew.

"I'm sorry, Finnegan, I wasn't able to get the stains out completely. I'm not sure what kind of wine it was, but it really dug in."

He nods and hands her a credit card. I notice a ring on his right hand. The symbol looks familiar, but I can't place it.

Tanya pulls a small device out from under the counter and lays the credit card in it. She places a slip of paper over the card and—

This can't be happening! I'm witnessing someone use one of those old credit card slidy machines from the eighties. It's like I'm visiting a pioneer village attraction where people still make their own candles and brooms. It's fascinating.

"See something you like?"

I might have leaned in a little more than I intended. The man's voice is too friendly and far too suggestive. I'd like to say something about how he's old enough to be my father, but if this is Finnegan Wells—and according to the slidy-device slip it is—I'd like to ask him a few questions. "I'm new in town. What's your favorite place for pie?" I may or may not have winked as I said this.

He smirks and looks me up and down. "I'll get a booth at Myrtle's on Main. Do you know the place?"

"I'm sure I can find it . . ." I pause for his name.

"Wells, Finnegan Wells."

"I'll be there in five, Finnegan." One more wink. Why not? You get more flies with honey, right?

He walks out and looks over his shoulder to stare at my rear end.

Yuck. I hope that's not what I look like when I'm lusting over Erick.

"How can I help you, Miss?"

"Hi, Tanya. My grams said you'd know what to do with this dress. It holds a special place in her heart and requires some TLC."

She looks at me like I'm crazy. "The dress I recognize, but have we met?"

Right. In her world my grandmother is dead. "Haven't had the pleasure, but my grams, God rest her, always said you were the best."

A relieved smile spreads across her face. "Any stains?"

"I don't think so. I only wore it for a couple hours. I tried to be careful."

She examines the dress with a shrewd eye and

peers at me over the half moons of her bifocals. "You've certainly done better than him. He brings that shirt in and tells me there's a wine stain." She shakes her head in disdain. "Forty years I've been in the business. I know a wine stain when I see one."

"I'm sure you do." I nod supportively. "What do you think it was?"

"I'll tell you what I know. That was blood if I'm a day."

I don't follow her analogy, but I go with it. "Blood? Why would he say it was wine?"

"Your guess is as good as mine. I suppose his girlfriend doesn't want him fighting anymore."

"Who could blame her?" Imagine that! He's got a girlfriend and he just invited me to pie. "Maybe I shouldn't meet him for pie, eh?"

Tanya laughs. "I wouldn't want to call down that woman's diamond-studded wrath." Her eyes go wide.

She clearly said something she regrets. I don't have enough information to know what, but I make a mental note to add an actual note to my phone as soon as I can. "When can I pick up the dress?"

"Monday okay for you?"

"Perfect. Thanks, Tanya."

I turn to leave.

"What name do I put it under? Isadora's account was closed when she passed, bless her."

"Mitzy Moon." I derive a secret pleasure from watching her lips mouth the name silently. Word does travel fast in a small town. Now she has a face to put with the rumor.

I hustle over to the diner and pray that I can catch Odell's eye before he blurts out a greeting.

Taking the slow and careful approach, I peer in the corner of the window. Finnegan is holding court with Tally, his back to the door. I can't see Odell. I take a deep breath and hope for the best.

I push open the door slowly and search the orders-up window for some sign of life.

Tally takes no notice of me.

Odell's face pops into the window and he raises his spatula.

I put a warning finger across my lips and shake my head. I nod toward the outspoken Finnegan.

Odell winks. "Tally, I need your expertise."

Tally nods to Finnegan, giggles at something he says, and sashays into the back.

I rush over and put a hand on Finnegan's shoulder. "I hope I didn't keep you waiting."

He tilts his head and grins up at me. The white of his teeth nearly blinds. I'm not sure if it's over-whitening or grossly mismatched veneers. Upon closer inspection, I also notice the too-even blackness of his monochromatic hair.

He stands and purposely brushes up against me as he gestures for me to take a seat in the booth.

"What do you recommend?" I dare to steal a glance toward the kitchen.

Odell and Tally have their heads together and she's whispering furtively.

"They have the best pin cherry pie in Birch County." He catches my eye across the table and winks. "I always have the pie."

"Oh, how quaint." I nearly gag on my own reply.

Tally approaches the table and struggles to avoid my eye. "What can I getcha?"

My companion stares at Tally with a look that I will dub "the buffet." This accurately describes how his eyes move up and down a woman's body as though he's starving and she's a multi-course smorgasbord for the pillaging. Oh, and let me add—yuck.

"I'll have the pin cherry pie, as usual, Tally. And don't skimp on the ice cream." He winks.

The wink is as over-reaching as if he had smacked her on the ass.

She looks down at the table and says, "And for you, ma'am?"

I giggle and say, "When in Rome."

Finnegan chuckles and winks.

Tally stares at me and shrugs.

"I'll have the pie and ice cream, too." I pretend to struggle to read her nametag. "Tally," I manage.

She grins and practically runs back to the kitchen.

Finnegan leans across the table and whispers in what must pass for sexy in his one-track mind, "Tell me about yourself." He punctuates the phrases with a little snap of his teeth.

Is it possible that he smells of scotch at two in the afternoon? I lean toward him in spite of my disgust and purr right back. "I'd rather hear what a powerful man like you does in a tiny little town like Pin Cherry." I try to lick my lip in a sexy way, but the bile rising in my throat nearly chokes me.

He doesn't notice.

"Big fish. Little pond." He leans back and props his arm across the back of the bench seat. "My family just about owns this town. The Wells men ran the iron ore business around here since before this town was even incorporated."

I would love to point out that the iron ore business dried up two or three decades ago, but more flies with honey . . . "Do you still run a refinery, or operate any of those big machines?" I bat my eyelashes to distract from my hideous delivery.

"We don't mine any ore these days. I'm more of a local entrepreneur and philanthropist." He spins the massive signet ring on his right hand.

If memory serves, every unemployed loser on reality TV refers to himself as an "entrepreneur." "How fascinating," I gush. "What sort of philandering do you do?"

He grins.

He thinks I don't know what I said. That pleases me deeply.

"Probably the biggest event I sponsor is the massive annual Halloween Masquerade. We convert the refinery into a mind-blowing haunted ball and raise a small fortune for charity."

"How exciting." I'm running out of exclamations of praise. "You said 'we.' Who can you trust to help you organize such an important event?" I cross my fingers under the table.

"Oh, no one plans a fundraiser like Kitty Zimmerman." His eyes glaze over for a moment and it seems he's enjoying a private mental picture.

"Don't you mean Zimmerman-Duncan?" I try to maintain an absolute innocence in my tone.

"Of course, of course." He looks at me with a hint of suspicion and perhaps concern. "Do you know Kitty?"

"We only just met today at the Duncan Club ladies' luncheon." I search my mental thesaurus for a word I can utter without choking. "She's stunning."

He leans back and smirks. "She's something, isn't she?"

"Mmhmm." I can't wait to tell Grams that I uncovered "the trollop's boyfriend." Check. Time to push a little harder. "So what charity?"

His eyes snap into sharp focus. "Beg your pardon?"

"I was wondering which charity you and Mrs. Zimmerman-Duncan support with all the money you raise?" I watch as his beady eyes dart left and right. I can almost smell the smoke wafting from the little gears in his cretinous mind as they whir toward disaster.

He shifts and the vinyl bench seat creaks under his sweaty backside. "I didn't catch your name?" His fake smile strains.

"Oh, it's Mitzy. Mitzy Moon." Once again I derive a sick pleasure from watching his lips mutely form the syllables of my name.

Tally sets down two slices of glistening red pin cherry pie with mountains of creamy vanilla deliciousness melting over the flaky pastry.

Finnegan's entire demeanor shifts from lascivious predator to threatened wild animal. "I don't appreciate being played." He slides out of the booth in a huff.

Tally scurries away.

I shrug and slide a slice of pie in for closer inspection. "Thanks for the recommendation. The pie looks delicious."

He leans down and his voice comes out as a scotch-tainted growl. "No one makes a fool of Finnegan Wells."

I raise a forkful of pie as though it is a glass of champagne. "Duly noted." I shove the whole bite in my mouth and let the ice cream dribble down my lips.

He glowers.

I wipe the drip with my thumb and suck the ice cream off. "See ya 'round, Finnegan." I flutter my remaining fingers in a "toodles" kind of wave.

He storms out.

I exhale, thank every foster care bully that toughened my hide, and fight to gain control of my racing heart.

Tally gasps.

Odell utters a low whistle. "It was like watching Myrtle come back to life."

I can't wait to get back to the bookshop and tell Grams all the good news. Including the bit about Odell's lovely compliment.

CHAPTER 17

WHEN I GET BACK to the bookshop the front door
is locked, so I fish out my key and let myself into the
store.

I don't know if I'll ever get used to the eerie silence, but the booktopian smell gives me an unex-
pected dose of comfort. When I close the door and
twist the locks, I actually feel "home." I haven't felt
that sensation since my mom passed. Venturing
north to explore the "great lakes" has turned out
pretty okay.

I cautiously make my way through the darkness
into the stacks and close my eyes. Today was a
rollercoaster, but having this place to come back to
gives me a solid feeling I've never known. Tomorrow, before anyone can show up and arrest me, I'm

going to walk along that narrow balcony edging the second floor and climb to the top of that teetering ladder. It's time for me to know more about this bookshop than anyone else. I'm going to start with the first book on the top shelf in the north corner and work my way through every precious tome in MY store.

Opening my eyes, I stretch out an arm to either side. The spines of books that could take me to other realms tickle the tips of my fingers and I sigh with satisfaction. No matter how tough things got, and whether the ends met or not, my mother always made sure I had a book to read.

A small flicker of light swirls toward me and expands. "How was that, dear?" She fades in and smiles.

"I didn't even pee a little, Grams. I think that's the one. That's the entrance I prefer."

Her melodious laughter sweeps over me and drifts into the stacks. She politely leaves my previous private thoughts untouched.

I pull out my phone and use the blue glow to guide my feet up to the apartment. "You aren't going to believe what happened at the cleaners."

She floats over to the bed, and the way she hovers it almost looks like we're having a sleepover. She appears to lie on her tummy, ankles crossed, with her chin resting in her hand. "Tell me every-thing," she gushes. A vision enveloped in Marchesa.

Inhaling sharply, I cover my mouth, and tears flood from my eyes.

Grams instantly whirls to my side. "What is it? Did someone hurt you?"

I imagine I can almost feel her ethereal hand rubbing my back. "It's nothing bad, Grams. I don't know what came over me. I looked at you on the bed with that attentive smile and—"

"Oh, honey." She wipes her cheeks. "I hate that I can't hold you, but I'm so glad I'm trapped in this bookstore."

We both laugh through our tears.

"I never had family like this—not since Mom, well, you know."

She nods.

"I didn't realize how lonely I was until I came to Pin Cherry Harbor. Aside from the arrest for mur-der, this has been the best few days of my life."

"That murder charge will never stick, dear." She flicks away the idea and claps her hands to-gether. "All right, enough touchy-feely sharing. What happened at the cleaners?"

I tell her about Finnegan Wells' bloodstained shirt.

"Make a note." She points to my phone.

Next, I mention Tanya's comment about diamond-studded wrath.

"Kitty?"

"It has to be, right?"

"I told you there was a boyfriend." Grams is positively glowing. "Didn't I tell you?"

"You did." I finish with the pie-related events at Myrtle's Diner.

"Odell always was quick on the uptake. Smart as a whip, that man." She smiles and her energy grows calm, as she seems to drift through her memories. "I'll never forget the day we opened that diner."

I must ask the burning question. "Why did you switch from Myrtle to Isadora?"

"When things ended with Odell, I truly felt like a part of my life and my heart were gone forever. Myrtle was the wide-eyed girl who fell head over heels for a young hero. When the drinking drove the wedge between us—"

"Odell's an alcoholic?" He seems so clear-eyed and steady.

Grams turns away and a long silence hangs between us. "Not Odell, dear. Not Odell."

"Oh."

She looks into my eyes and nods. "Oh, indeed. My second marriage was a non-stop party. When the car accident took Max from me and left me with a limp and one kidney, the light finally came on. I dropped 'Myrtle' and all her mistakes. Isadora got sober, went to meetings, and formed a stable relationship with a responsible man—Cal."

"I had no idea."

"Of course you didn't. Water under the bridge, dear." Grams gives me that Midwestern stiff-upper-lip look.

"Now I understand why you left Odell the diner in your will."

"He never remarried, you know." Grams touches a tiny silver band on her left hand.

Never one to get too comfortable with raw emotion, I launch into the *coup de grâce* of my meeting with Finnegan. "Anyway, he mentioned that same Halloween ball and how much money they raise for charity. But, get this, when I asked him the name of the charity he got all bajiggity with me."

"I have no idea what that means, honey."

"Oh, right. He became defensive, and said, 'No one makes a fool of Finnegan Wells.' Then he gave me a threatening glare and stormed out."

Grams fans herself and breathes a sigh of relief. "What did you do?"

"I ate the pie. I'm not an idiot."

She laughs so hard ghost snot comes out her nose.

My chest swells with pride.

I'm too exhausted to go through my dad's case files, so I treat myself to another ridiculously perfect hot shower and collapse into bed.

CHAPTER 18

PYEWACKET'S ROUGH TONGUE attempts to lick my eye open. I toy with the idea of ignoring him, but the recent memory of his pointy teeth on my earlobe causes me to roll out of bed.

I stumble to the bathroom and Pye rubs against my legs, nearly knocking me off my unsteady feet. "Let me wake up, son."

Shockingly, Pye immediately ceases his assault. His tufted ears twitch and he leaps to the top of an antique armoire near the secret door. His head tilts and a dangerous look sharpens his gaze.

Wood scrapes against wood as the bookcase slides open.

I step back into the bathroom and peek around the beveled molding.

The door is completely open, but no one enters.

A disembodied voice utters a stern warning. "Robin Pyewacket Goodfellow, if you deign to lay one claw upon my head I'll turn you into a mouse."

Pye hisses.

Silas enters. "Pardon the unannounced early morning call, Mitzy. I have much to discuss."

I stare. Clearly I need coffee, but did I just witness Silas and Pye having an actual conversation? I mean, Pye seemed to know who was coming, and Silas expected the attack. I rub my eyes and yawn loudly.

"Lovely," murmurs Silas. "May I escort you to breakfast at the diner?"

"Gimme two minutes."

"Please, take five." Silas gently lowers himself onto the scalloped-back chair and Pye appears directly under the ready fingers of the attorney. The tufted ears relax and the gnarled fingers scratch. They have the comfortable air of old friends.

I shake my head and close the bathroom door. A splash of water, a rinse of mouthwash, and skinny jeans swapped for my leggings. I'm ready to eat.

I cross the room and Silas leans back and squints. "What's this now?" He gestures to my tee.

I look down and shrug. "It claims that abstinence is only 99.99% effective." I point to the graphic. "It's the Virgin Mary and baby Jesus. Get it?"

Silas cocks his head to one side, and a flash of amusement touches his milky-blue eyes. "I do. That is quite humorous."

He could've simply laughed, but I suppose stating the fact of something's hilarity is another way to go. "Ready for breakfast?"

"Indeed." He rises from the chair.

"Hi-ssss." Pyewacket launches through the open bookcase and down the stairs.

"I better give him his Fruity Puffs. I'd hate to see what those claws could do if he gets impatient."

"Lifetimes of indulgence. He'll never learn." Silas shakes his head.

I hurry after the wildcat.

When I come out the front door of the book-shop, Silas is working levers and sliding the gearshift in the Model T, but there are no sounds of its sputtering engine. I lean in and suggest, "How 'bout we walk the two blocks?"

Silas mumbles something, ostensibly to the car, and exits his vehicle. "Very well."

There's only one booth left in the bustling diner and Odell doesn't notice us when we enter. My goodness, this must be the weekend rush—but it's Friday.

Silas leads the way to the booth and Tally arrives before I can slide in.

"You best get your orders in right quick. Those

three tables just sat down, but I can slide yours in ahead of them if you know what you want." Her bright red bun bobs anxiously.

"Bring us two specials and some black coffee." Silas nods his dismissal.

"I might not want the special, Silas. And I take cream."

"We'll need to address your trust issues," he mumbles.

I take offense, but keep it to myself. "Why is this place so busy on a Friday?"

"It's opening day of the Pin Cherry Festival. I hope you've asked Twiggy to assist you at the bookshop."

What makes him think I would've asked Twiggy to assist me during a festival whose existence I only just uncovered? I let it lie and move on to neutral territory. "You said we had a lot to discuss. Did you get a copy of the medical examiner's report?"

He nods. "The amended report."

"New time of death?"

"Originally, based on decomposition and insect activity, they claimed Wednesday morning between 10:00 and 11:00. However, after the forensic pathologist reviewed the tissue samples sent to the county crime lab—"

I lean forward.

"—the corrected time of death is Monday night between 8:00 and 9:00 p.m."

I lean back and slap a hand on the table. "Kitty said she hadn't seen him since Monday."

Silas places two fingers on my hand. "Decorum, Mitzy."

"Is our local ME a hack?"

"Not in the least. However, at county they discovered a strange striation in the cells that indicated the body had been frozen immediately after the murder. The extreme temperature slowed decomposition and gave a false time of death."

I glance around and catch several people as they look away. I lean in and lower my voice. "There's no way I'm a suspect now, right?"

"Unfortunately, no one on the bus remembers you, and the ticket alone isn't an airtight alibi. However, I do think Sheriff Harper is finally pursuing other avenues."

"Like the avenue of how the skanky widow and her boyfriend knocked off my grandfather for his money?" I tap my pointer finger on the table —lightly.

"Evidence points toward Kitty. What's this about a boyfriend?"

I whisper, "I think there's something going on between her and Finnegan Wells." I suddenly recognize the symbol from Finnegan's ostentatious signet ring. "Plus, he was wearing a ring with the Duncan family crest on it."

Silas steeples his fingers and his eyes travel to a place I can't follow. "Interesting. Quite interesting."

"What? Did I solve the murder?"

Tally gasps at the word and clatters our plates onto the table. "I'll—um—coffee." She scurries off.

I look at the plate in front of Silas and see an egg-white omelette with green peppers and cheese. No toast. No potatoes. My heart sinks as I shift my gaze to my own plate. I have a pile of fluffy scrambled eggs with chorizo and jalapeños, two slices of sourdough toast, and a golden-brown mound of home fries. "How did we both get the special?" I point to our two completely different breakfasts.

"That is what is special. Odell always knows what you want."

I grin like a fool and look toward the kitchen. Odell gives me an amused nod before he jumps back into filling orders.

Tally places two steaming mugs of java on the table and slides a little melamine bowl filled with individual creamers toward me. "Thank you." I pour a good deal of thick, rich cream into my coffee and slide the bowl toward Silas. He waves it off and continues with his report.

"The business I had to attend to involved a conclave with Cal's lawyer. There were some matters between his estate and Isadora's that needed set-tling. She mentioned that Cal had come to see her Monday morning and requested some drastic changes to his will. The alterations would have left Kitty with a mere fraction of what she'd been promised."

"Whom was he leaving everything to? I mean, Grams died before him so—"

"He was moving Jacob into the primary posi-tion and you as the contingent."

"Me? Why me? I thought he and my dad were estranged. I don't understand."

"Nor do I, Mitzy, but this information regarding Finnegan Wells intrigues." Silas scrunches up his large nose.

"Did I mention the Halloween Masquerade?" I ask. "He said that they, he and Kitty, raised a small fortune for charity every year, but when I asked the name of the charity he got all bajig—I mean, irri-tated and left." Silas tilts his head and I add, "Plus, Tilly said the loan on the iron ore refinery had been paid off."

A slow smile pushes up Silas's sagging cheeks. "You are far more than a barista, Miss Moon. Far more."

CHAPTER 19

I WALK BACK to the bookshop alone. I may be slipping down the suspect list for Cal's murder, but
that fails to lift my spirits. Silas promised to set up a
meeting with my father and that prospect has me on
edge.

I stop and stare at the line forming in front of
Bell, Book & Candle. I definitely need Twiggy.
Crap! I don't even have her number—or a phone
with service. I'm rich now. I should definitely
handle my cell-phone inadequacy.

I cross the street slowly, tossing around various
delay tactics, when a familiar cackle reaches my
ears.

"Right on top of the poor sheriff. I'm telling
you—"

"You certainly are." I interrupt Twiggy's recounting of my crash landing on Erick at the diner and shove my special key in the lock.

Murmurs and snickers close in around me. This is not the day I had planned. I pull open the large door and Twiggy and her acolytes stream through without so much as a glance at their benefactor—or a thank you. I give a little harrumph and march to the back room.

Twiggy holds up a bank pouch and nods. "I took the liberty of grabbing the drawer money. I knew you'd be swamped with the Pinners."

I want to wallow for a few more minutes, but she's actually pretty thoughtful. "What are Pinners, dare I ask?"

"Out-of-towners that come up once a year for the Pin Cherry Festival." She shakes her head.

"This is the first I'm hearing of the Pin Cherry Festival," I say with more bite than I intend.

"Easy, doll. I'm sure there's still time to put your name in the hat for Princess of the Pin Cherry Festival, if that's what's got you so wound up."

"You know what?" I don't bother to finish the thought. I grab Pye's box of Fruity Puffs and march up to the apartment without another word.

Once inside my hideout, I sputter all kinds of snappy retorts.

"Since your lips are moving, I'm gonna jump in."

I shove a handful of cereal into my mouth and crunch loudly.

"Didn't you just come from breakfast?"

"I stress eat when I'm not stress drinking. Don't judge."

Grams puts her hands up in surrender. "Two things, dear: Pyewacket's wrath will be merciless if there are no Fruity Puffs for tomorrow's breakfast."

I remove my hand from the box and search the high places for furry retribution.

"And Twiggy will bend over backward for you if you show her a little respect."

"She was entertaining a crowd with stories of my misfortune."

"Are you saying landing on top of Erick Harper was unfortunate?" Grams winks.

I giggle and blush. "Hardly."

We both laugh.

"I was hoping to spend the day going over Dad's case files. I didn't know there was a princess pageant and a cherry jubilee!"

"You're too funny, Mitzy." Grams floats toward the settee and repeats, "Cherry jubilee. Delightful." She settles into a reclining hover. "Just run down and let Twiggy know how much you need her help and that you have to review the case. Piece of cake, dear."

"Is there a bakery in town?"

Grams looks at me as though I've lost it.

"You said cake, and I thought 'yes' and now I want cake."

"Take the Fruity Puffs downstairs and clear your schedule. We need to—"

"Cal was changing his will," I blurt.

Grams shoots up toward the ceiling. "Cereal. Schedule. Case." She ticks off the list on her bejeweled fingers and hurtles toward me. "No time to lose, Mitzy. No time to lose."

The sight of Ghost-ma barreling directly at me lights a fire beneath my feet. I hustle back downstairs.

Grams was right, of course. Twiggy is more than happy to take the reins for the day and that leaves me free to delve into my father's history and find the real killer.

By the way, I've pre-decided he's not guilty. But there's a method to my madness. People always say that if you only have a hammer you'll always find nails. I'm paraphrasing. So, it stands to reason that if I assume innocence I'll find the proof. I know, pure genius. Right?

The bookcase barely slides closed before Grams swoops in with questions. "Did you say Cal was changing his will? Why on earth would he do that? Do you think he knew about Kitty and Finnegan?"

I wave my hand wildly to get her attention. "I

only know what Silas told me. He met with Cal's attorney to settle some business between your estate and Cal's and the attorney said she met with Cal on Monday to discuss the changes. Of course, Cal never returned to sign the new documents."

"What were the changes, exactly?"

"Silas said Cal was giving pretty much everything to Jacob and then me as something called a contingent."

"To Jacob? You must've misheard, dear. Cal disowned Jacob after the murder conviction. He never would've put him in the will . . . unless . . . "

"Unless what? Unless what, Grams?"

"You better dig into those files, honey. And you better search Cal's office tonight to see if he left any clues that would tell us what changed his mind about Jacob."

My eyes widen. "Search Cal's office? I'm sure it was just an end-of-life, no-regrets kind of thing. You know, like you putting me in your will in spite of my dad's edict."

"Sweetie, I knew I was dying. I had time to put my affairs in order. Cal was murdered. There has to be another reason he wanted to leave things to Jacob."

"Good point," I concede. "But I'm no cat burglar, or any kind of burglar. There's no way I can break into Cal's office tonight."

Grams swooshes past me and hovers above the vanity. "Oh, you don't have to break in, Mitzy dear. I have a key in the secret compartment of my jewelry box."

Secret doors. Secret compartments. My Grams could be mistaken for a shady character.

"I beg—"

I point to my lips and shake my head.

"Fine. Let's see if you can find the compartment without my help."

I sit down at the marble-top vanity and pick up the tiger-maple jewelry box. I carefully inspect all sides and the bottom. I open the lid and then slide the latch to the left. A thin drawer pops out the right side.

Grams gasps. "How did you know?"

I force myself to think of anything besides how I discovered the trick. I don't want her to have the satisfaction of hearing my thoughts.

A ring in the top compartment catches my attention. I slip it out from between the smooth rolls of purple velvet for a closer look.

Grams silently moves closer.

I hold the ring toward her. "I like this one. It has a cool dome-y shape."

Her reply is barely a whisper. "It's a cabochon."

I lean in and ask, "I heard something about a Shaun."

She clears her throat. "Cabochon. That's what the shape of the stone is called. It's just an old mood ring I picked up at a pawn shop in the seventies."

"What's a mood ring?" I ask as I run my finger along the twisted gold rope surrounding the stone.

"Why don't you put it on?"

Something in her voice makes my pulse race. I slip the band on the ring finger of my left hand and twist it back and forth.

She continues her explanation. "The stone changes color depending on your mood. I can't remember them all now, but purple meant that you were feeling romantic, and I think brown or grey meant your were nervous. Some rings had pink, but—"

I hold up the hand bearing the ring and look at my grandmother.

She stops in midsentence. "What is it, dear?"

"What does black thunderstorm tornado mean?" I swallow hard.

She zooms in. "What?" She tries to touch the ring but her ghostly fingers pass right through my hand. "Darn it! What do you see?"

I pull my hand back toward me and stare into the ring.

The room disappears. Everything is black. Energy is swirling around me like flashes of lightning. I call out to Grams, but no one answers.

I feel a powerful need for alcohol. I feel intense love for my son. I feel a desire for power—and knowledge. I feel sorrow over my divorce. I miss Max.

My head is spinning. These aren't my feelings. "Grams! Help me!"

I collapse.

When I open my eyes Grams is hovering above my body, calling my name. I can't hear her voice, but I can see the panic in her ghostly face.

"Take off the ring," she cries.

I hear that! I whip the possessed ring off my finger and drop it on the floor. I push myself to a seated position and take several shaky breaths. "What the heck happened?"

"Did you have a vision?"

I shake my head. "That's a pretty random question, Grams." I exhale and tell her about the blackness and the feelings.

"Maybe it's hereditary," she mumbles.

"What's hereditary?"

"I used to get visions and premonitions—when I was alive. But it seems like you might be clairsentient."

"Who's Claire?" I hold a hand against my left temple. "I'm so dizzy."

"It's not a who, it's a what. Clairsentient means that you can feel other people's emotions, and you get messages through them. Sometimes you can even feel things beyond the veil."

I tilt my head and look at my grandmother like she's lost her mind. "So, you're saying I can feel dead people?"

She nods. "Maybe."

Apparently, my clever *Sixth Sense* reference is lost on her. "What's happening to me?"

"I honestly don't know, dear. We can talk to Silas about it tomorrow. For now, I think it's best to get a drink of water and distract yourself with the case."

I open my mouth to protest, but then an odd thought tumbles in. "Grams, why would I want to talk to Silas about this?"

She turns away and, if I didn't know better, I'd say she's acting a little cagey. "Oh, you know, he reads all those books in the loft. He has a wealth of arcane knowledge."

I'm too woozy to battle Ghost-ma. I walk to the bathroom and slurp some water from the faucet.

"Honestly, Mitzy." Grams shakes her head.

"I'd never make it all the way down those swirly stairs to get a cup." I wipe the dripping water with the back of my hand. "Now, where were we before I had my episode." I attempt to chuckle, but it makes my head throb.

"You were getting the key to Cal's office." Grams helpfully points toward the jewelry box.

I look suspiciously at the Pandora's box, but I'm anxious to shift my focus to something I understand. "Which key is it, and why do you have a key to Cal's office?"

"It's the brass key that says 'Do Not Duplicate.'" She snickers. "It doesn't say anything about 'Do Not Keep.'"

"And the why?"

"Oh, he gave me a key when we were married. I must've forgotten to return it after the divorce." Her innocent ghost eyes widen.

"Mmhmm. Thing is, Grams, I can't imagine that the key still works thirty years later." I turn the key over in my hand. "He may have even moved his offices."

"Never." She shakes her head. "Cal Duncan's family has owned the Midwest Union Railway since his great-great-great-grandfather drove the first spike through the rail where the tracks begin down by the docks. The president and chief engineer's office has always been in the top floor of the Pin Cherry Harbor station. And Cal never changes something unless he has a real good reason. If it ain't broke, don't fix it was his favorite motto."

"Then he must've had a real good reason to change his will," I mumble.

"Exactly," Grams says, emphatically. "So, you'll search his office tonight?"

I rub the letters etched into the key and surmise that breaking and entering should carry a lighter sentence than murder. Plus, technically it's not "breaking" if I have a key, right?

Grams confirms my thoughts with a nod.

"All right. Let's put that on the back burner for now and dive into Dad's case."

"10-4," says Grams.

I chuckle and hunker down next to the stack of witness statements. There's still nothing useful here. I go back to the list of evidence. "It says Dad had a 9mm in his possession at the time of the arrest and Darrin had a .45. I'm no expert, Grams, but I can't imagine that ballistics could confuse those two rounds. They pulled a 9mm slug out of the victim."

"Jacob didn't do it. A mother knows."

I'm not sure how to respond, so I continue with my summary. "And a 9mm slug from the damaged security camera in that room." I lie back on the floor and look through my hovering grandmother. "All the witness statements claim to have heard two shots. Two 9mm slugs. Dad had a 9mm. I'm not seeing the magic bullet, Grams."

"Read the police report out loud. I always used to read my screenplays aloud when something wasn't working."

I sit up and stare, dumbfounded, at the ghost. "You wrote screenplays?"

"Oh, dozens. I never got to make a film, though. Such a shame. All that talent and the world will never have the pleasure." She sighed.

"I went to film school, you know."

She shakes her head. "I didn't. Would I have seen any of your films?"

I shrug. "I dropped out and only worked on a few short films and commercials before selling my soul to the exciting world of coffee."

"All our experiences make us who we are, dear. The choices you made brought you to me." Grams smiles warmly.

I always looked at my life as a series of regrets, but if things had turned out differently . . . I may not have been so eager to escape my life in Arizona and venture off to great lakes and mysterious harbors. I basically failed "up." That's called the Peter Principle.

A stifled chuckle escapes from my ghostly matriarch.

I playfully shoo her away. "Enough personal reflection. We need something to investigate." I pace in front of the open file boxes and wait for lightning to strike.

"You said both of the recovered bullets were 9mm, right?"

I nod and continue to wear a path in the plush Persian rug. "The rifling!"

"I thought you said it was a 9mm not a rifle, dear."

"Think about every cop show you've ever watched, Grams. They always prove that a bullet was fired from a specific gun by doing a rifling test." I crouch down and sift through the reports in box number three. "That makes no sense . . ."

Grams swoops down. "What? What is it? You're not giving me anything!"

I drop the report and stare through Grams. "The ballistics report says that the bullet recovered from the camera matched the lands and grooves on Dad's gun."

"Well, he always said he was the one who shot out the security camera."

"Right. The problem is the bullet they recovered from the victim didn't match."

"Was there a third gun? You said Darrin had a .45."

"No, it's not that. The other slug was smooth. There was no rifling at all."

"Is that possible?"

"I'm not an actual detective, Grams." I stand and resume my path. "Who do we know that knows stuff about guns?"

"Sheriff Erick?" She snickers.

I like that she's calling him Erick too. "Who do we know that won't arrest us for having boxes of evidence 'borrowed' from the records tech at the sheriff's station?"

"Of course, dear." Grams swirls around and I wait. I barely know anyone in Pin Cherry. I certainly don't have a list of everyone's hobbies.

Grams seems to be thinking out loud. "Cal had some hunting gear, but that 9mm that Jacob stole was his only handgun."

"What about Odell? He kinda looks prior military."

"Yes! Good eye, dear! Odell did a short stint in the Army before we married. He was an Army chef. That's how we got the idea to open the—"

"Grams, focus." I snap my fingers and interrupt her reverie.

"Odell is our best bet. Maybe you can grab some lunch and ask him a few questions."

"Lunch? Wow, I totally lost track of time." As if to scold me, my stomach growls audibly.

"Run along, Mitzy. I'll be here when you get back."

CHAPTER 20

THE DINER IS PACKED with Pinners and I'm forced to take a seat at the counter. The round, red-vinyl-covered stool scrapes a little as I spin to face the kitchen.

Odell looks up, gives me a knowing nod punctuated by promising a sizzle.

Tally slides a soda, or rather a pop—the local term—in front of me and keeps walking.

The woman has stamina. My best guess is that she's in her sixties and she never slows down. I take a sip of my soda and snippets of conversations waft into my consciousness.

"Kitty always has the best party of the festival."

"Such a shame about her husband."

"I heard some vagrant murdered him in an alley."

"You don't say!"

The Duncan-blooded part of me wants to make a scene and tell them all to shove their gossip where the sun don't shine, but the curious part of me hopes to overhear something useful.

Tally sets my plate down and winks.

I look up and catch Odell's eye. "I need to talk to you," I shout.

"I'll take my break when you finish. So, in about two minutes?" He chuckles and throws down another batch of burgers.

He's not wrong. I devour the juicy burger and french-fried pieces of perfection in roughly two minutes.

"Tally, kitchen's on a break," he calls above the din of the busy restaurant.

I bus my dishes and follow Odell out the back door. This has to be the cleanest alley I've ever seen.

"What's on your mind, Mitzy?" He pulls out a beat up cigarette and puts it in his mouth.

I wait for him to light it.

He does not.

"What's going on there?" I point to the unlit smoke.

"Oh, I quit fifteen years ago."

I raise an eyebrow and gesture for him to continue.

"I carry one around in my pocket and put it in my mouth when I take my breaks. Reminds me what it took to give it up—how far I've come—that sorta thing."

"Doesn't it make it harder?"

"You'd think, but I've always liked to prove to myself that I'm stronger than average."

"That why you joined the Army?"

He grins. "Who told you that?"

I clearly can't tell him the truth. "Just a lucky guess." I point to the haircut.

He rubs a hand over his grey buzz cut and nods. "What can I do ya for?"

I chuckle. "How folksy."

He nods. "Not that I don't enjoy your company, but . . ." He pokes his thumb back toward the busy diner.

"I'll get to the point. I have a gun-related question and someone said you'd be the person to ask."

"Boy, seems like your lucky day," he teases.

"I'm looking into my dad's old case—no one knows except Twiggy—and I found something odd."

"Shoot." He chuckles.

"They recovered two bullets from the crime scene. Both 9mm. The one they pulled from the destroyed camera had rifling that matched my dad's gun."

He nods. Seems like everyone knows the details of this small-town murder.

"The wackadoo thing is that the one from the victim's wound was smooth."

"Perfectly smooth?" Odell tilts his head.

"That's how the report makes it sound. No rifling, but it was—well, it was cause of death for the store manager, so it had to be fired."

"Boy, that never came out in the trial."

"Really? Do you think the cops suppressed it?"

"I doubt it was intentional. Two 9mm bullets. One perp with a 9mm gun. I s'pose they figured if one matched that was close enough. They were under a lot of pressure to convict quick." Odell shook his head. "Small towns never like scandals."

"Do you know what would've caused it?"

Odell slips the raggedy cigarette back in his shirt pocket and shakes his head. "I've got some Army buddies who know a little too much about guns. I'll ask around."

"But don't say anything about my dad's case," I caution.

He points to his grey hair and says, "I wasn't born yesterday, kid."

"Thanks, Odell. Grams said—" I freeze and my eyes dart around like pinballs.

He leans back and narrows his gaze.

I have no idea how to cover that slip. I figure a

good old-fashioned ramble and run is my only option. "I better get back to the bookshop. It's so busy." I continue to stammer nonsense as I yank open the back door and escape through the diner.

I practically sprint, emphasis on practically, back to Bell, Book & Candle. Grams is waiting right inside the main entrance and I start babbling as soon as I see her, utterly oblivious to the stares and whispers.

"I'm sorry, Miss Moon, you'll have to repeat that. I didn't quite hear you." Twiggy walks toward me and levels a concerned stare.

I slap a hand over my mouth and hop over the "No Admittance" chain before she, or I, can say another word.

Grams surges through the bookcase and is swirling anxiously in the bedroom by the time I make my way through the secret door—human-style.

"Sorry about that, dear. I didn't think you'd start talking the minute you saw me."

"My fault. I was all flustered because I slipped up with Odell. I couldn't stop myself from blurting as soon as I walked in the bookstore." I smack myself in the forehead. "Stupid."

She ignores my self-deprecation. "What do you mean 'slipped up?' What did you say to Odell?"

"He was super helpful and said he'd ask some

Army buddies about the weird bullet. I kinda blurted 'Grams said' before I could stop myself."

"Did he hear you?"

"Oh he heard. He heard." I pace from the four-poster to the secret door.

"Water under the bridge. We can't cry over spilt milk."

Laughter grips me. "A bird in the hand . . . a stitch in time . . . " I laugh so hard tears come to my eyes.

"Well, I never." Grams crosses her arms and shoots up to the ceiling.

"I thought we were just shouting out proverbs." I wipe the happy tears from my eyes and catch my breath. "Regardless, it will be a day or two until we hear back from Odell. Where does that leave us?"

"Don't you mean irregardless?"

I take a deep breath and prepare to launch into my well-rehearsed speech on this pet peeve, when Grams zips down to the Persian rug, laughing all the way.

"Well played. Well played." I like this comfortable banter with my Ghost-ma.

She chuckles in spite of our no-mind-reading rule. "To answer the question you asked out loud, it leaves us with a pressing need to search Cal's office. Are you able to do that tonight?"

Before I can answer, Twiggy's disembodied voice interrupts.

"Mr. Willoughby is here, Mitzy."

I look at Grams. "What the heck is that? Can she hear everything we're saying?"

"It's an intercom, dear. Over there next to the bookcase." She floats toward the secret door. "See this fancy scrollwork? It covers the speakers, and these mother-of-pearl inlaid buttons are the way to respond. The one on the left lets you talk and the one on the right is the 'call' button to ring the back room. The middle rings the museum."

That reminds me that I haven't seen the museum yet. Maybe tomorrow. I push the button on the left. "Can you send him up to the apartment?"

"You have to take your finger off to hear her reply," Grams prompts.

"—his way, doll," is all I catch, but I get the gist.

"Does Silas know about you?"

Grams looks at me and shrugs. "Does he know about you?"

"We're not talking about me."

Grams lifts a finger to protest.

I silence her with a shake of my head. "I'm not ready to talk about the incident. Is that clear?"

She nods obediently.

"Now, back to my question. Does he know

you're hanging around the bookshop like some kind of afterlife mascot?"

"Oh, that." She hesitates and doesn't make eye contact. "Let's see if he picks up on anything."

"And if he doesn't?"

"What are you getting at, honey?" She looks pensive.

"Do I tell Silas that the ghost of my dearly departed grandmother hangs out with me in the apartment?"

"It's not hanging out, Mitzy. I'm trapped in between. I can't leave the bookshop for some reason. I'm just making the best of things."

I open my mouth to take offense at that last bit, but the bookcase slides open and Silas fixes me with a disappointed look.

"Good morning, Mitzy."

He makes no effort to hide his distaste for my preferred name. "Hey, Silas. What brings you up to the clubhouse?"

He glances at the papers strewn about the floor. "Any progress?"

I bring him up to speed on my suspicions as Grams swirls closer.

Silas stiffens and steps past me. "I feel a chill. Do you have a window open?"

I raise an eyebrow in her direction and she

snickers. "Maybe it's a sense and not see thing, like Pyewacket."

"Maybe," I reply.

Silas looks at me as though I'm daft. "Maybe? Are you reporting that you are unable to recall if you raised a sash?" He looks down the row of casements. "They appear to be secure."

Grams swirls closer.

Silas shivers. "Do you feel it right now?"

He pulls a pair of round spectacles out of his coat pocket and holds them in his right hand. He murmurs something I can't quite make out and hooks the curved brass bows behind his ears. As he peers through the taffy-tinted lenses, a slow smile spreads across his lined face. "Ah, Isadora. I had hoped it was you."

My face goes slack. I can't help but wonder what just happened!

"Silas is an alchemist, dear."

I gaze back and forth between my Ghost-ma and my lawyer-turned-wizard and can't find a single syllable.

"Can you communicate with her?" asks Silas.

I close my mouth, swallow, and—

"Mitzy, he can see me now, but he can't hear me. Maybe it will take some time . . . I don't know how this works. You have to bring him up to speed."

I continue to search my brain for word bits.

"Sweetie, Silas is the one who uncovered the information in one of my wonderful books. He's studied the rare books since I began collecting them and he convinced me I could find a way to wedge myself between the worlds and have a chance to meet you."

I manage to force out a single word, "Yes."

He smiles up at Grams, and she presses her hands to her ghost-chest in a pantomime of gratitude.

I find my voice. "Are you a wizard?"

Silas chuckles and coughs. "I'm an alchemist. It's the study of mystic and scientific transmutation of matter. Some people confuse it with wizardry. Some might even be inclined to label me a warlock; however, I would protest such nonsense."

A memory leaps forward. "That day in the hospital! When you touched my gunshot wound and I stopped bleeding . . . Was that magic?"

"It's not magic, Mitzy. Through the knowledge I've gathered, I'm able to make permanent changes to the state of matter." He smiles warmly.

"Sounds like magic to me."

Grams floats between us. "It's not magic, dear. I'd say it's more philosophical than spells and potions."

"It sounds like magic to me, Grams."

Silas's sagging cheeks perk up. "You can truly

communicate. Magnificent!" He claps his hands together and nods. "We did it, Isadora."

A happy glistening of tears wets the corners of his eyes, and despite my confusion, I can't stop myself. I hug Silas tightly. "Thank you. Thank you for giving me a chance to know my grandmother."

He stiffens uncomfortably, clears his throat, and steps away. "You're quite welcome. Now, I came on business." He takes off the round spectacles and slips them back in his pocket. "I've arranged a meeting with your father."

"Oh." Now that he's scheduled something, I'm not entirely sure I'm ready to meet dear old Dad. I'm looking into the case, and I hope he's not guilty, but what if he is?

"You know your father didn't do this, Mitzy. You have to meet him and hear his side." Grams flickers in and out. The powerful emotions must be draining her or something.

She has a point. I'm pretty certain my dad didn't commit the murder, and I've lost everyone else in my life. What have I got left to lose? "I'd like to hear his version of events."

Silas nods.

"When do we meet?"

"How about breakfast tomorrow at that dining establishment you prefer?"

"Myrtle's Diner? That seems too public. I might cry or yell or—"

Silas offers another option. "How about in the museum, after breakfast? Perhaps 10:00?"

"All right. I'll see you both tomorrow."

Silas puts on his spectacles, smiles at Grams, and says, "That gown and that age suit you, Isadora. Until tomorrow."

She waves.

As the door closes behind him, I fire off a few inquisitions. "Um, why didn't you tell me about Silas and the alchemy? Why didn't you mention you planned to stick around after death? And how on earth did you and Silas come up with this crazy plan?"

After hours of question and answer regarding rare books, magic, alchemy, and the afterlife, I'm temporarily out of queries. I reserve the right to re-open the investigation at any time.

Grams agrees to my terms.

Back to the business of my current investigation.

"Tell me again how this thirty-year-old key to a penthouse office is going to work?"

Grams explains the layout of the train station/office complex for Midwest Union Railway and how easy it will be for me to gain access to Cal's office.

"Now, I haven't been there in years, dear, but they never had any security or anything. Pin Cherry is a safe town."

Except for Cal's murder, I guess.

We agree to disagree on the relative safety of the town and enter the holy closet to select the proper attire for prowling. I vote for all black, but Grams wisely points out that I don't want to look like a burglar.

In the end, we agree on a charcoal-grey Donna Karan pantsuit with a lilac blouse.

"You'll look like you belong there. If anyone is there after hours, they won't think twice about a business woman with a key to the place." Grams nearly pats herself on the back.

"If anyone is there after hours, I'm going to rip out of there like a cat with its tail on fire."

Pyewacket gives a soft hiss from his perch atop the antique mahogany armoire.

"Oh Mitzy, so dramatic." Grams rolls her eyes.

I plug my phone in. I've seen enough movies to know that a fully charged battery is essential for spy photography. "Do you have a thumb drive, Grams?"

"Is that a gardening tool?"

I chuckle. "It's to save files from a hard drive."

"You've lost me, honey. Just take pictures."

My spy kit is shy a few nifty gadgets, but I resign myself to reality and wait for sunset.

CHAPTER 21

THE NARROW STREETS around the train station are utterly deserted. I drive by several times to make sure there are no cars in the parking lot.

It seems the only folks out at this time of night are a few die-hard locals at the dive bar, Final Destination, down by the docks.

Once I satisfy my nerves, I park my rather obvious silver gull-wing Mercedes two blocks over and walk back to the Midwest Union Railway building.

I slide the key in the lock in the back door and whisper a prayer as I apply pressure to the key.

CLICK!

No way. Grams will never let me forget this. I carefully open the door and tiptoe down the hallway, searching for the steps up to Cal's office.

I get turned around a couple times, but eventually find the stairwell Grams described and gain access to the office with my handy master key.

The room is impressive. Enclosed in thick, gleaming glass, Cal's office looks over the entire train station. The converted building houses office space, conference rooms, a break room, and part of the original terminal has been preserved as a display housing a shining steam engine.

I close the door and lock it. Again, I've seen the movies.

I reach for my phone and panic. I pat myself up one side and down the other and stifle a scream. I left my flipping phone on the charger!

New plan. If I find something important —take it.

I choose a methodical search pattern. Framed photos. Bookcase. Desk. Trash.

I make my way around the Viking statue in the corner and move to the photos hanging on the one section of wall that is not glass. The light from the few after-hours fixtures in the station cast enough illumination for me to make out the faces. Two family photos from my father's early years. I chuckle at the likeness of the Isadora in the photos to her current form. She does indeed look similar to the ghost that haunts my bookshop. The third image is a hunting-trophy shot with Cal, a moose, and another man I don't recognize. The fourth picture is much older. Cal looks about twenty, and he and three buddies are all bunched together for the camera. They each have a cigarette hanging from the corners of their mouths and they are all in military uniforms. Army, I'm guessing. Before I turn away, something grabs my eye. That man next to Cal—

I inhale sharply. I'd recognize that buzz cut anywhere. The hair might be several shades darker, but that man next to Cal is absolutely Odell Johnson.

Funny, Odell never mentioned they served together. I make a mental note to ask Grams if she knew.

The bookcase holds a few small art pieces, several awards, and hardbound volumes that seem to be all for show. In fact, one has a hollowed-out spot for a flask. Nice touch. But a thorough search doesn't turn up any secret messages or hidden keys.

I pass the trash can on my way to the desk. Not to jump out of order, but the waste bin is empty.

The desk has been cleaned and organized. Possibly the sheriff, but more likely a secretary. Cal was apparently too modern to have a paper desk calendar and someone has taken his computer. I go through the drawers.

Nothing of interest in the top drawers. The right file drawer contains a bottle of D'Aincourt Cognac Premier Cru. The matte black bottle with raised metal insignia rests in a custom wooden case.

Grampa Cal's fancy. It's irresistible. I have to take a sip.

It smells like baked pears with cinnamon. The taste of vanilla, nutmeg, and luscious fruit warms my whole tummy. Good gravy! So, this is how the other half lives.

I have one more sip. It's beyond words.

I reluctantly replace the bottle. Didn't Grams say they met at AA? Maybe Kitty drove him back to the bottle? I shrug and continue my search.

The left file drawer contains a few manila folders with notes for supplier meetings and one with receipts.

I sit in my grandfather's cushy, ergonomic leather chair and sift through the slips of paper. Lunches, dinners, fishing trips, hunting lodges, and a—private investigator?

A noise from downstairs startles me. I shove the PI receipt in my bra and put the file folder back in the drawer.

If I hide under the desk and get discovered I'll look guilty. If I walk around the room like I own the place—

I move toward the books on the shelf when the beam of a flashlight hits me right between the eyes.

"Don't move. I'm going to need to see some identification."

Great. Sheriff Erick.

He fumbles with the handle. "Miss, I'm going to need you to unlock this door, or I'll be forced to break it down."

I saw the thickness of the door and I'm certain he has no chance, despite his burly shoulders and powerful legs. However, I also know that he's a little trigger-happy, and I don't want another accidental bullet wound. No point in testing the breadth of Silas's skills.

"Don't shoot, Erick. I'm opening the door."

"Miss Moon? I didn't recognize you."

I open the door.

He holsters his gun and stares at me.

I choose to take this as progress.

"How did you get inside that locked room?"

He doesn't know I have a key. Time to think fast. "I came up earlier to get a feel for the kind of man my grandfather might've been. I guess the secretary didn't see me sitting in here in the dark. She just locked me in. I'm awfully lucky you showed up. I could've been stuck in here until day shift." I pat him gratefully on the back as I slip past and head to the stairs.

"Just a minute, Miss Moon."

I stop, but don't turn.

"The door unlocks from the inside."

Darn! He's got me there. "I must've forgotten with all the emotion of being in my grandfather's office and knowing I'll never have the chance to meet him. I wasn't thinking straight." There, that sounds like a solid girlie reason.

"You wouldn't be poking around in Cal's murder case would you?"

"Me? I just own a little bookshop. Before that, I was a barista. Hardly sounds like the pedigree of a crack detective." I start down the steps.

He hurries to catch up, and the scent of his nearness gives me a little infarction.

"If you happened to stumble across something you'd let me know, wouldn't you, Moon?"

The sound of my name on his lips . . . "Have you hit a dead end in the case?" I reach the bottom of the stairs and turn. "You don't still suspect me, do you?" I reach out and adjust the nameplate above his badge.

"Is that alcohol on your breath? Have you been drinking?"

Oops. "My grandfather had some lovely cognac is his—office. I just drank a toast to his memory." It's best not to mention the bottle was in the desk. I don't want him to think I was snooping.

"I see." He looks me up and down.

I shiver and smile. "You didn't answer my question, Erick. Am I still a suspect?"

He swallows twice and looks everywhere except at me. "You're not our primary suspect, but we haven't found evidence that knocks you completely off the list."

"There's a list? Whose company am I keeping, Erick?"

"I can't discuss an ongoing investigation."

"Swallow once for yes." I lean toward him. "Is Kitty on the list?"

He swallows and steps back.

"How about Finnegan?"

He swallows again. "Let's clear out of the train station, Miss Moon." He steers me out by my elbow.

I step out to the parking lot and chew the inside of my cheek. Maybe he'll drive off and I can walk to my cleverly concealed car without his notice.

"Assuming you only had the one drink, can I give you a ride to your car?"

My eyes widen.

"I observed it parked over on Chokecherry Lane. This is the third building I cleared."

Awww, he was worried about me. "Like I said, lucky you found me."

He chuckles and opens the passenger door of the patrol car.

At least I'm sitting in front this time. That's progress, too.

CHAPTER 22

I QUIETLY LET myself into the bookshop and make my way without the aid of light. I wish I had my phone.

I am gaining some familiarity with the place, and I'm rather proud that I've made it to within sight of the chained staircase without—

CRASH!

A tumble of books hurtles to the ground behind me and I scream.

Grams appears out of nowhere. "What is it? Is someone after you?"

I hold a hand to my heaving chest and thudding heart. I gasp for breath and reply, "No idea. I don't see—"

A single sound pierces the night. "Reow."

Of course. The demon cat, out for some late night fun. "That cat tried to kill me."

A ghostly snicker tinkles through the darkness.

"It's not funny. I could have a weak heart. Those frights could be deadly." I stomp off to the back room and flood the bookshop with light. "Now, let's see what kind of mess he's made this time."

Grams ghost-pets the purring CAT-astrophe while I clean up.

I put a few books back on the shelf before I recognize the pattern. "What are you doing with all these books about guns in your bookshop? A US Army technical manual?" I slide it into place. "Or *The Theory and Design of Ammunition*?"

"I don't recall adding those to the collection, dear. Sometimes Twiggy picks things up at estate sales. You'd have to ask her."

I look from the book in my hand to the pesky fur-covered terror. Did he knock these down on purpose? I shake my head, but keep the ammunition book all the same. "I'll take this upstairs for a little light reading."

Pyewacket purrs loudly and bounds up the steps ahead of me.

"That's a good kitty," coos Grams.

"Please don't encourage the tan terror."

A phantom throat clearing cuts the silence

when I drop the Donna Karan suit on the floor, but I choose to ignore it. Instead, I climb into the heavenly bed, click on a bedside lamp, and open the weaponry treatise.

Soon the tantalizing lull of dreamland—

A furry torpedo knocks me awake and possibly fractures my floating rib.

The riveting text on bullets, sub-projectiles, and grains per pound times the acceleration of gravity had lulled me into a lovely sleep. I was right in the middle of a magnificent dream starring Sheriff Erick when kitty-bomb attacked.

"Anything?" Grams floats next to the bed.

"I can't keep my eyes open." I lay the book on the bedside table and snuggle in for the night.

Pye kneads his claws into my shoulder.

"Shove off." I give him a tentative push. I want him off, but I don't want to draw his wrath. "I'll keep reading in the morning with a strong cup of coffee and—some Fruity Puffs, if you don't let me sleep."

Pyewacket growls softly, but parades to the end of the bed and curls up like an angel.

Cut to—angel falls from heaven, directly onto my chest, and I wake up gasping for air.

"I'm up. I'm up." I push the comforter and Pyewacket off my scared-to-life body and stumble to the bathroom.

"Are you up already?" Grams calls from a modest distance.

"Yes, apparently I couldn't wait to jump back into that enthralling book." I gesture toward the manual on the nightstand and see Pye stretched across my pillow with one insistent paw resting on the spine.

As soon as I make eye contact his tufted ears twitch and his hefty paw slides.

The book thunks to the floor.

"I said I'm going to read it!" I throw my hands up.

"He needs his breakfast, dear. And you need some coffee." Grams swooshes through the wall as she mumbles, "Not a morning person."

"I heard that!" I open the bookcase and Pyewacket rockets past, knocking me sideways.

I pour a bowl of Fruity Puffs for him and one for myself.

Pyewacket gives me an "if looks could kill" stare.

"Just this once, Pye. I haven't had time to get to the market."

He ignores me and eats.

I push "brew" on the coffeemaker and munch the cereal while I wait for my go-go juice.

Steaming mug in hand, I climb back up to the apartment.

Two cups of coffee and one argument with Pyewacket later, I've actually found something. "This sounds promising . . ."

"Do tell, dear."

"There's a thing called a sabot. It's made out of plastic and can hold a bullet inside the barrel."

"Isn't that where all bullets go, honey?"

I drop the book on the bed and sigh. "I'm not explaining it right. If I understand all this technical mumbo jumbo, it means that you could shoot a small bullet out of a bigger gun."

"And?" Grams circles her hand impatiently.

"Well, technically, Darrin could've placed a 9mm bullet in one of these sabot thingies that fit into his .45-caliber gun. That would explain the lack of rifling on the second 9mm bullet."

"What about the third shot?"

"Maybe there wasn't a third shot. I keep reading Darrin's statement and it seems like the mysterious third shot was how he explained the gunpowder residue on his hands. But the police never found a third bullet or the missing security tape."

"If there was no third shot—if Darrin fired the shot that killed—"

It's hard to watch a poltergeist cry. "This is good news, Grams. This means it's actually possible that Dad didn't kill the store manager."

"That's why I'm crying, dear. We turned our

184 / TRIXIE SILVERTALE

backs on him. We let him rot in jail." The tears turn into full-blown weeping. "What kind of mother must I be?"

"Grams, you can't blame yourself. The police didn't even figure out what Darrin did."

Pyewacket adds his mournful call to the keening.

After years of hiding my pain from taunting foster siblings, I don't "do" emotion too well and I can't imagine how to begin comforting a ghost. I slip into black skinny jeans and a "Hot Mess No Stress" tee with a stack of syrupy pancakes pictured.

The mourning duo doesn't acknowledge my exit. Fine by me.

I hustle down to the station.

"Is the sheriff in?"

"Whom may I say is asking?"

Wow. This clerk has to be the only person in town who doesn't know me. "Tell him Mitzy Moon has urgent news."

Her eyes widen and one eyebrow does a comical arch.

Now that is the reaction I've come to expect.

She picks up the phone and delivers my message.

Sheriff Erick rounds the corner, looks down at my T-shirt, grins, and shakes his head.

I shrug and follow him back to his office.

"What's the urgent news, Moon?" His smile is warm and his gaze lingers.

I toy with the idea of saying I had a dream about him, but I need him to be cooperative and I want to engender some good will. I'll save that little gem for later. "I promised I'd share any information with you and I'm here to keep up my end of the bargain."

Surprise tainted with suspicion paints his handsome face.

"I think Darrin MacIntyre killed that store manager."

Erick leans forward and confusion floods his expression. "I thought you were here about Cal's case?"

"Not today." I smile innocently.

"Well, the protests of a long-lost daughter are expected, but that case was decided many years ago. In fact, your dad's already out of prison. Why would you point the finger at Darrin now?"

Anger rises faster than I can tamp it down. "Are you saying that it's all right for my father to serve a fifteen-year prison sentence for a crime he didn't commit just because he's out now?"

Sheriff Erick leans back.

"Are you saying that my dad should carry the label 'murderer' around for the rest of his life when there's a better-than-average chance he's innocent?" I take a deep breath and power up for more.

Erick stands and puts his hands up. "Easy, Erin Brockovich. Why don't you tell me why you think he's innocent and we'll take it from there."

I look down to see that I'm standing and waving my hands like a nut job. Deep breath. One more for good measure. I lower my arms and sit. "Are you aware the bullet that was recovered from the victim didn't have rifling."

He narrows his gaze. "Where did you get that information?"

"Did you know or not?" I sidestep his question.

"I wasn't on the force back then. Rookies hear rumors, but I never saw any evidence to support that claim." He leans forward. "Have you?"

"Let's assume I have." Feint and parry. "If that were the case, is it possible that Darrin MacIntyre fired the kill shot from his .45 by using a sabot to jacket the 9mm bullet?"

He shifts his sexy jaw back and forth. "Where are you getting your info, Moon?"

"Oh, Pyewacket got me a book on guns and ammo." *Touro!* I swish my imaginary bullfighter's cape. I slip by without answering another query.

I can see by the look on his face that what I've proposed regarding the use of the sabot is possible. That's enough. I stand and smile. "Thank you for your time, Sheriff."

He opens his mouth, but I twist on a dime and rush out like a hipster to an artisanal cheese shoppe.

I'm tempted to stop at the diner for a proper breakfast, but a flash of nervous tummy hits me and I hurry back to the apartment.

I'm going to meet my father in less than two hours. I should probably shower.

I peel off my tee before the bookcase closes.

"What's the hurry?"

"I'm freaking out about meeting him."

"Jacob? Oh, he'll love you, dear. Don't worry about a thing."

"I'm freaking. It's what I do."

"Where'd you go?" Grams pats under her puffy eyes. "Pye and I didn't see you leave."

"I ran my theory past Erick. He wouldn't answer, but I could see by the look on his face that it's possible."

Grams disappears into the closet. "I'll find you something lovely to wear."

Why argue. I unhook my bra with one hand while I twist the hot water on with the other.

A slightly sweaty, crumpled piece of paper falls to the bathmat.

I pick it up and smooth it out on the counter. Oh yeah, in the flying book fiasco, I forgot all about the PI.

Grams bursts through the wall from the closet. "What PI?"

I grab a towel to cover myself. "Grams, rule number two: no phase-shifting into the bathroom without an express verbal invitation."

She giggles. "Number two, in the bathroom. You're a stitch, Mitzy."

She vanishes back through the wall, still giggling.

I'd close the door, but what's the point?

I slip under the glorious spray of water. Hot, steamy showers will never get old.

I wrap a thick cottony towel around myself and sit down at the vanity to attempt a replication of the makeup I applied for the ladies' luncheon.

"You look lovely, dear."

I go for a more casual version of the sleek hairdo that Grams had supervised, but I use product and a blow dryer all by myself.

"Come and see what I've picked out."

Grams heads through the wall and I walk around, like a civilized person.

"Where is it?"

"I can't actually move anything, honey. I'll point and you grab. These boots." A pair of knee-high, black-leather riding boots

I nod approvingly.

"And I thought this sweater with your own

jeans." She points to a chic black-and-grey-striped cashmere boyfriend sweater.

I touch the soft knit and purr appreciatively. "This will look great with skinny jeans."

"I thought you'd like to pair it with something of your own. To feel grounded in yourself."

"Kinda woo woo, Grams."

"I was just trying it out. Seemed like something you kids would say."

"Not this kid." I put on the outfit and look at myself in the full-length mirror. "Do you think he'll like me?"

"How could he not, dear? You're his daughter." She brushes a tear from her cheek.

"You should've been buried with a handkerchief, Grams."

"Oh, Mitzy." She laughs. "You're too much."

I walk to the secret door and turn to look up at Grams. "Ready?"

"You want me to come?"

"Can you?"

"I actually haven't tried to go into the museum. I'll be there if I can."

"All right. But don't say anything. I'm crazy nervous already. If I start talking to ghosts in front of him . . . Just be there for moral support."

"You got it."

I walk out into the Rare Books Loft and the

bookshop actually has customers milling around on the first floor.

"It's on the third shelf at the end of the self-help stack." Twiggy's knowledgeable yet impatient voice drifts up to my ears.

Good to know that's being handled. Now I need to figure out how to get into the museum.

Grams floats down to my side and winks. "Follow me," she says.

I guess her thought-hearing comes in handy in a crowded room.

Near the double-stacked rows of windows at the front, there's a grey metal door marked "Employees Only." Man, I have got to get familiar with this place.

Grams fades through the door and pops just her head back toward me. "Looks like I can access the museum." She slips out of view.

I depress the metal push-bar and follow.

A new world. The smell of ink, metal, and history.

The space is only half the size of the bookshop, but it has an entire second floor rather than balconies and a mezzanine. The ground floor houses large equipment in a variety of historical displays. "Is that an actual Gutenberg press?"

"I'll give you a full tour later, dear. I hear Silas."

I turn to face the door I just passed through.

There's a scrape as the metal bar is pushed. The door swings open— My chest constricts. I can't breathe. Beads of sweat pop out on my forehead.

"Breathe, dear. Focus on me and breathe." Grams hovers between the opening door and me.

My heart races, but I manage to gulp down some air.

Silas walks through first. His balding head, thick grey mustache, saggy cheeks, and baggy brown suit give me a strange sense of calm.

The man behind him is tall and handsome. His close-cropped, ice-blonde hair is the exact hue of my own, and his piercing grey eyes lock onto me with intense worry.

"Mizithra?"

Years of emotions agitate in my gut like a washer on spin cycle. Longing. Hate. Anxiety. Fear. Disappointment. Loss. Abandonment. Love. "Dad!" I lose all sense of modesty as I close the distance between us, and despite the fact that I promised myself I would not cry, I sob into his blue cotton shirt.

His strong arms engulf me and I feel safe, safer than I've ever felt in my life. I wish my mom could've felt this safe.

"Thank you for agreeing to see me." His raspy voice is barely a whisper.

His voice is thick with emotion. He actually

thought I might not agree to see him? This poor man. I squeeze my arms around him. "I can't believe you're real."

I swipe the flood of tears from my face and assume that my careful application of makeup is caput. But I don't care, because my dad is alive. I'm not an orphan.

He leans back and looks down at me with so much love I might melt. His voice catches a little as he says, "I can't believe you're here. What have you been doing since you got to Pin Cherry?"

Before I can reply, Grams swirls in and blurts, "Tell him about the sawb-oh thing and how we think he's innocent—and that wicked Darrin—"

I wave my hands. "Give me a second, Grams. My world is spinning for the third or fourth time this week. I'll tell him everything in a minute. Gimme a second to process."

Silas grins. "Isadora never had the gift of patience. I see that hasn't changed."

I look at my dad and my shoulders sag. We just met and I'm hearing voices. He'll probably disown me on the spot.

"Silas brought me up to speed on the way over. I'm not sure if I believe in ghosts, but if anyone could find a loophole in death, it would be my mother." He glances around the room and announces to the air in general, "I'm sorry I wasn't at the funeral, Mom. I didn't think the town would take too kindly to my return."

"Tell him I love him. And tell him we know he's innocent."

"She says she loves you." I shrug self-consciously. "And I'm not sure if Silas mentioned it or not, but we've been looking into your case and we think we can prove that you didn't commit the murder."

He shoves his hands in the pockets of his faded jeans. "I guess we're jumping right into it then." Jacob takes a deep breath and walks to the front windows.

"We've lost too much time already," I offer quietly.

He nods and stares into the distance. His fingers wipe absently at the dust on the sill and he exhales.

I want to ask a million questions about the time he spent with my mother, if he loved her, and if he ever thought of me, but the best way to give him a fresh start is to clear his name. I plow ahead. "Darrin shot the guy, right?"

Jacob laughs, but it's a bitter, humorless sound. "I stopped saying that after my first nickel in lockup."

I walk over and put my hand on my dad's arm. "Look, I'm not going to pretend I understand what it's like to serve a sentence for something you didn't do, but I got accused of murder about an hour after I arrived in this town. You lost fifteen years of your life. You want to give up the rest of it, or are you gonna fight?"

He has to pull himself back from a faraway place. It takes a moment for his eyes to fully focus on me. "Who accused you of murder? Whose murder?"

"Sheriff Er—Harper arrested me for Cal's murder."

Jacob shoots Silas a worried look. "Why didn't you tell me about this?"

Silas shrugs. "She's been all but eliminated. He's moved on to questioning Kitty and Finnegan Wells."

"Kitty," grumbles Jacob.

"Do you know anything about the interrogations? Did they admit to the fake fundraising?" I walk toward Silas as I fire questions.

"I delved into the 'charity' that benefits from the Halloween Masquerade philanthropy and your suspicions were correct. It funnels through several convoluted pipes, but in the end it lands in Finnegan's pockets."

"And what about the affair? Is he seeing Kitty?"

"Apparently, she vehemently denied it, but phone records provided evidence of a suspiciously high number of calls between the two." Silas shakes his head.

Grams swishes down and gives me a sanctimonious grin. "I told you it was the trollop."

"So, they did it? Did Cal find out about the affair? Is that why he was changing his will?" I slap my hands together. "Of course, Kitty must've found out about the will and convinced Finnegan to kill Cal before he could make the changes official."

Jacob raises his hand like a schoolboy. "May I ask a question?"

I don't want to pause, but I gesture for my father to speak.

"Who said Cal was changing the will?"

Silas steps into the fray. "I spoke to your father's lawyer earlier this week. It seems Cal was leaving the bulk of his estate to you."

"Me?" The color drains from Jacob's face and he looks left and right. "Me? He hasn't spoken to me since the gavel fell and they carted me off to prison. What on earth would possess him to put me in his will?"

Before any of us can speculate, the metal "Employees Only" door opens and two anything but employees walk through.

Deputy Paulsen already has her weapon trained on my dad. "Don't move, convict."

"Sheriff, what's this about?" My father's face reddens with anger.

I chime in with, "Erick, what's going on?"

Sheriff Harper pulls out his cuffs. "This is standard procedure when dealing with ex-cons. Everyone keep calm. Kitty Zimmerman-Duncan claims she was having an affair with Jacob Duncan. Obviously we have to follow every lead in a murder investigation." He walks toward my dad. "I'm not putting you under arrest, I'm—"

"Arrest? You think I killed my own father?" Jacob looks like a trapped animal.

His eyes snap to the door and I sense his need to escape.

I feel it in my gut, just like when I had my episode with the mood ring. I rush forward.

"Freeze, scumbag." Deputy Paulsen points her gun straight at my heart.

"Dad, don't worry. We know you're innocent. We'll find the proof. Please don't do anything stupid."

He shakes his head. "Seems like the only stupid thing I did was come back to this backwoods piece of—"

"Dad, don't make it worse." Despite the firearm zeroed in on my torso, I reach out and place a hand on the sheriff's arm. "Erick, it's only questioning. Can you please skip the handcuffs? He'll cooperate." My eyes plead with the sheriff. "You'll cooperate, right Dad?"

"Sure, for you. I'd do anything for you." His voice is barely a whisper.

The knot in my stomach fades.

Jacob's shoulders relax.

Erick slips the cuffs back in the holder on his belt. "Don't make me regret this, Jacob." He takes him by the arm and they walk out.

Silas follows and adds, "Please note that my client is represented by counsel, Sheriff."

Deputy Paulsen brings up the rear and mumbles a familiar refrain, "The guilty always lawyer up."

CHAPTER 23

SILAS DRIVES OFF to meet my father at the station, but I decide to walk. I have a stop to make.

I push open the door of the diner and the lunch crowd is packed in like sardines. Every seat is full, and Tally's daughter delivers food while Tally takes orders. My timing isn't great.

I slip back into the kitchen and the smell of burgers instigates a loud growl from my stomach.

"Should I throw one down for ya?" asks Odell.

"No thanks. I've gotta get over to the station."

He looks up and raises an eyebrow.

"Long story. I'll be back for lunch after the rush."

He returns to flipping burgers and drops the basket into the fryer. Popping, snapping, and bubbling welcome the raw potatoes into the oil.

I push the hair back from my forehead. Geez, it's hot back here. I guess I'd have a buzz cut too if I had to work over a grill all day. "How come you never mentioned that you and Cal served together?"

His spatula stops mid-slide. "That's none of your business, kid. Twiggy shouldn't be tellin' tales out of school."

I have no idea what he means. "Twiggy didn't say a thing. I saw a picture of you, Cal, and a couple other guys in uniform. The photo was hanging in Cal's office."

He doesn't look at me. "Why were you poking around in there?"

"Odell, what's going on? Did something happen between you and Cal?"

He plates up a few orders and refills the fry basket for the next batch. "I won't speak ill of the dead, Mitzy. That's all I'm saying on the matter. Your grandmother and Cal are together now." He scrapes his metal spatula across the grill and I barely hear his last comment. "That's how it should be."

He can play coy all he wants. I happen to have direct access to one person in that triangle, and I've never known her to keep quiet. "Thanks, Odell."

"See ya later, Mitzy," he calls through the orders-up window as I leave.

I walk back to the bookshop.

Grams is nowhere to be found. I think as loud as I can while searching the apartment. No response, and no sign of Ghost-ma.

If at first you don't succeed, try, try . . . the best friend.

Twiggy rings up several books for an eager customer, wraps them in gold tissue, and places them in a black paper bag with a gold embossed Bell, Book & Candle logo on the side.

"Thank you. I just love this bookshop." The happy customer takes one more look around before she walks out.

"Twiggy, have you got a minute?"

She scans the stacks before she replies, "They can live without me for a couple minutes."

And modest, too. Once in the back room, I launch straight in. "I saw a picture of Odell and Cal serving in the Army together. I asked Odell about it and he said he wouldn't speak ill of the dead. Can you shed some light?"

"Did you ask Isadora?"

"I can't find her."

Twiggy nods. "Must be something going on, you know, on the other side."

I spare Twiggy the explanation of this in-between place where Grams is trapped and wait for a reply to my question. "Do you know anything?"

"I know everything, doll. If your Grams gets peeved about me telling this story, she better not haunt me. All right?"

"All right." I answer with a confidence I don't possess.

"Your Grams was a USO gal and she and Cal really hit it off."

"But I thought Odell was her first husband?"

"Am I tellin' this story or are you tellin' this story?"

"Please continue," I say with a bow.

"Anyway, the boys got shipped off, and Myrtle promised to wait for Cal. Odell came home first and he looked her up straightaway. Myrtle was a free spirit and a bit of a drinker back then. She had a few too many, woke up next to Odell, and claimed true love."

"I can relate," I mumble.

"They did seem to be in love. She had a bit of money saved and Odell had saved his Army pay, too. They had a quickie wedding, bought the diner, and dove into their new life."

"But they ended up divorced."

"Clearly. Did you want to hear why?" Twiggy takes a stack of bags and ties little gold ribbons on the handles while she talks.

I nod silently.

"Cal returned from his deployment a year later,

and when he came callin' on Myrtle he discovered that his best friend had stabbed him in the back. Things got ugly fast. Myrtle drank while Odell and Cal fought. She divorced Odell and ran away. I lost touch with her during the Linder years—that was the second husband. She traveled the world, partied with the rich and famous, and lived dangerously. When Linder died in a car crash five years later, she got his fortune. The accident shook her up. She got sober and dropped her first name."

"Wow."

"I'll say. When she came back to Pin Cherry as Isadora Linder, Cal pursued her relentlessly. They had a fairytale wedding. Odell and Cal never spoke again."

"But Odell spoke kindly of Grams when I came to town."

"He swears Cal broke them up, and he never blamed your Grams for any of it. He never remarried because he claimed he still loved her, but there was always bad blood between him and Cal."

"How bad?"

"After Isadora died, Silas had to contact you before he could make the details of the will public. But in the meantime, Cal tried to buy up the diner and the bookstore. Tally said he and Odell had a knock-down, drag-out in the diner a few weeks ago."

"Does Erick know about this fight?"

"The whole town probably knows. Why?"

"Well, wouldn't that make Odell a suspect?"

"Odell? He wouldn't shoot anyone."

"Twiggy, he was in the Army."

"Sure, doll, but he was a chef."

"Wait, how do you know Cal was shot?"

"I hear things." Twiggy shrugs.

"Did you happen to hear the caliber of the bullet?"

"Nah, I'm a little deaf in one ear, you know." Twiggy grins and returns to the floor of the bookshop, just in time to help a customer who sounds desperate to locate a first edition of *Captains Courageous*.

I have first editions. This day keeps getting weirder.

Heading toward the stairs, I stop and pretend to browse when a snippet of gossip grabs my interest.

"I heard the owner passed away recently."

"How is it still open?"

"I'm sure it's something with the missing will. I saw Janice at the pie judging, and she said no one knows if there's a new owner. The whole place might shut down."

"What about all these books? Oh my goodness, it breaks my heart."

"Did you hear about the murder in—?"

That's my cue to leave. Maybe I'll put my name in the hat for Pin Cherry Festival Princess. Despite my notoriety as a murder suspect, it sounds like folks need to meet the new owner of Bell, Book & Candle.

I chuckle while I make sure the coast is clear. Good, no one on the mezzanine. I pull the candle handle and slip into the apartment.

I could go through my dad's case files one more time, but it seems pointless. I only have the one lead, and I need to wait for Odell's Army buddies—

The PI! Don't ask me to connect the dots. I run to the bathroom and grab the receipt. It's the weekend, but private investigators probably answer their phones seven days a week. I know I would. That reminds me, I'm definitely going to get my cell service re-activated on Monday.

I scan the apartment for a phone. There's a landline in the back room downstairs, so I thought there would be a line up here.

I don't see anything. I'm about to open the bookcase and look for Twiggy when the fancy scrollwork covering the intercom speaker catches my eye. Hooray!

I press the button on the right.

Nothing.

I press it a little longer.

Nothing.

I press it for longer than necessary.

"Yes, Your Highness?" Twiggy replies.

I don't care for her tone. "I was wondering if there's a phone up here?"

"Do you see a phone?"

This woman knows exactly how to push my buttons. "The lack of visual discovery is the reason for the call."

"Don't get your panties in a bundle, doll. It's in the privacy booth."

"The what now?" I look around the room and nothing stands out.

"Notice that bump-out in the far left corner, beyond the bedside table and the flapper display?"

I stare at the flapper and grin. There must be some juicy stories in my family's past. But I don't see the "bump" that Twiggy mentioned. "No, I don't see anything."

"Trust me, it's there. Anything else?"

I don't reply. How can she ask if there's anything else when she didn't address the first thing? Geez!

I walk to the far corner, past the flapper, and see that the wall comes out in a square. I assumed there was a chimney or some ducting running up the wall of the building.

I press on the wall and to my surprise—not as much surprise as a secret bookcase door or a Ghost-ma—the wall springs open to reveal a well-lit, cozy phone booth.

I step in and it takes me a minute to figure out rotary dialing. Once I solve that mystery, I dial the number on the receipt.

"Hello?"

I expected more. "Um, hi. Is this Jackson Investigations?"

"You called me."

Does he mean yes? Does he mean no? "I did. I was wondering if we could meet?"

"You got a case? I ain't got time for chit-chat."

Maybe this guy is related to Twiggy? At the very least they both went to the same finishing school. "Yeah, I got a case."

"Be at the diner in an hour."

The line goes dead.

I can't meet him at the diner. If Odell is somehow involved . . . I dial the number again. The clickety-swish of the rotary phone is growing on me.

"Hello?"

"Yes, hi. We just spoke and I can't meet you at the diner. Is there someplace else?"

"The pizza place on 87th."

"Wait, wait." I don't know much about Pin Cherry, but I'm fairly certain there's no 87th. "What city are you in?"

"How'd you get this number?"

I look down at the address on the receipt. Crap-tastic! This guy is in Minneapolis. "I'm calling from Pin Cherry Harbor."

He's unusually slow to respond. "How'd you get this number?" This time there's a menacing growl to the tone.

"Look, I'm Cal Duncan's granddaughter. I'm not sure if you heard what happen—"

"This conversation is over."

DIAL TONE.

That went well.

I step out of the booth and press the wall-door closed.

I'm sure that sheriff trumps PI. Looks like I'll have to share my lead with Erick if I want to get this private eye to talk. Fiddle-farts.

I wipe the smeared mascara from under my eyes and walk to the station.

Maybe I should ask if they have a punch card. Ten punches and I earn a date with the sheriff. Now there's a frequent-felon club I'd gladly join.

CHAPTER 24

THE INFLUX OF TOURONS—MY clever compound word for tourist/morons—from down south has pushed the small sheriff's station to its limits. A frantic lady in red has misplaced her handbag or maybe it was stolen; she's not sure. There are four teenagers arguing with a deputy about how the bottle of pin cherry wine got into their car without their knowledge. There's a large man with an impressive handlebar mustache that claims his pin cherry pomade stand was robbed.

I make a beeline for the desk clerk.

"Hi, I'm here to—"

She looks up from her game of Furious Monkeys and recognition flashes across her features, instantly replaced with disdain. "They're in interrogation room one." She points, dismissively. "Down that hall."

"Thank you." Let the record show that at least one of us has manners.

I approach the room and my hand hovers above the tarnished handle. Should I knock? I do.

"Come in," says Erick.

I smile and open the door.

My father looks up and shakes his head.

Silas looks more grim than usual and his shoulders seem to bear an additional burden.

"What's going on?"

The three men exchange a glance that has meaning only to their special trio.

"What?" I repeat.

Sheriff Erick stands and offers me his chair. "Close the door, Moon."

I close the door, but sitting seems like giving up. "I'll stand."

"Suit yourself." Erick returns to the chair.

"Can someone tell me what the heck is bringing down this room?"

Silas for the win. "Miss Moon, the sheriff has far more evidence than we assumed to support Mrs. Zimm—"

"Just call her Kitty," I interject.

"To support Kitty's claim of an affair." Silas pats my father on the shoulder.

"Of course. But the affair was with Finnegan Wells."

"We looked into that, but Mrs.—Kitty came forward with evidence to corroborate her claim that Finnegan was blackmailing her, and that she was actually having an affair with your father."

"She's a liar." I slam my hand down on the table.

"Easy, Moon." Sheriff Erick gives me a stern look.

Luckily I remember why I came to the station. "And the PI can confirm all this?"

The various versions of shock that pop up on the faces of the triumvirate are priceless.

"What private investigator? Hired by who?" Sheriff Erick leans forward.

"By whom," I correct. "I'm sure your thorough investigation included questioning the PI Cal hired. The one certainly hired to tail Kitty." There's a wonderful joke in there, but I must press on. "There are probably pictures of the dirty deeds committed by her and Finnegan that will clear my dad in a second. But I forgot, this town isn't about clearing my dad. Seems like you're all way more interested in suppressing evidence if it facilitates a speedy conviction."

"Mizithra, that's enough." Jacob puts his large, calloused hand on top of mine.

"It's Mitzy, Dad." I pull my hand away. "So, what did the PI have to say, Erick?"

"It's Sheriff Harper, Miss Moon. It sounds like you have some information you failed to share."

I know the words are meant to fill me with guilt and shame, but when I look at the muscles clenching in his rugged jaw I get all warm and gooey instead. I slap the receipt on the table. "I'm sharing it now. I spent my time wisely in Cal's office."

He picks up the slip of paper, reads the imprint, and looks me dead in the eyes.

My knees wobble.

"I could arrest you—"

"Save it for an actual criminal, Sheriff." I take my dad's hand. "Come on. We're walking out of here until the sheriff comes up with something besides the lies of a cheating hussy."

Silas grins briefly and smooths his mustache with a thumb and forefinger before schooling his features back into brooding introspection.

Jacob looks up and smiles. "Thank you, Mitzy."

I pull the door open and hold it for the men as they leave. I look over my shoulder and give Erick a wink. "Oh, and you're welcome." I add a little extra wiggle as I strut out of the station.

Dear lord, baby Jesus, I hope that PI doesn't have pictures of my dad with Kitty!

212 / TRIXIE SILVERTALE

Silas stops on the sidewalk and turns toward me. "I see potential in you, Mitzy."

But based on his recent revelation, the comment fills me with more trepidation than pride. "As an investigator?"

"As many things." He smiles and leaves us.

Way to vague it up, Silas.

Jacob sighs and says, "I could use a burger."

My eyes snap from the departing alchemist-attorney to my father. "Did you say that out loud or is my stomach reading minds?"

He chuckles and slings an arm around my shoulders. "Come on, let's see if Odell will serve me."

"Or me," I add. My last conversation with Odell didn't exactly end with balloons and streamers.

The lunch rush has cleared out and Tally eyes us nervously as we slide into a booth.

I smile and wave her over.

She approaches slowly. "Hi, Jacob."

"Hi, Tally. It's good to see you're still the brightest pin cherry in town."

She blushes and pulls a pencil from her flame-red bun. "What can I getcha?"

He smiles warmly. "We'll have two cheeseburgers, two cokes, and we'll split an order of fries."

Tally's eyes widen and she looks at me with concern.

"I'll have my own order of fries."

She sighs with relief. "That sounds better."

Jacob chuckles. "Sorry about that. I suppose I have quite a few things to learn about you. I'll make a mental note regarding not sharing fries."

"If there were a cardinal rule, that would be it." I sit back and stare at my father. The complications of Cal's case and the unresolved issues of my dad's old case all swirl haphazardly in my head. But my mouth takes a different route entirely. "Why did you leave Mom?"

"Whew!" He swallows. "You get right to the point, huh?"

"I figure we've lost twenty-one years. Why waste time on small talk?"

"Can't argue with that."

Tally slips the drinks onto the table and hurries away.

"The truth is, Mitzy, your mom and I never were together. It was a weekend fling and we didn't even exchange numbers."

I unroll my bundle of flatware and stare at the fork.

"I didn't find out about you until you were almost five. It was a fluke. I was back in Phoenix on railroad business and I thought about that amazing weekend so many years before and drove up to see the red rocks."

I swallow my hurt and fold the corners of my napkin into the center.

"I went poking around the old haunts I'd explored in Sedona during that college trip—and there you were."

I look up for a second, but the emotion bubbles too close to the surface. My napkin requires immediate attention.

"You and your mother were having ice cream in a place that used to be a sushi bar. I saw your hair—those eyes . . . I knew."

I fold the napkin ferociously and force myself to staunch the waterworks. I can't look at him, but I can't keep it inside. "Why didn't you say something to us? I think she was always waiting for you to come back."

"Maybe or maybe not. Truth is, she had my name and knew where I was from. If she had wanted me in your life she could've tracked me down."

I open my mouth to protest, but maybe he's right. Maybe it was all my childish wish for a father that I projected . . . Too much psychobabble. "Didn't you want me?"

His hand shoots across the table and grabs mine. "I was a disaster. It was right after I got back from that trip that Cal fired me. He'd already cut off my allowance when I dropped out of college, so losing the job was the last straw. I made a stupid plan with Darrin. You know the rest."

"But Mom died. I was all alone."

"I'm not saying I made the right choice, Mitzy. But I couldn't let you find out that your dad was a convicted murderer. You deserved better."

"What changed?"

He tilts his head.

"Why did you agree to meet me now?"

"According to Silas I didn't have a choice. He said either I come with him or he would give you my address. The way he described your, um, tenacity . . . Let's just say I wanted to come quietly and on my own terms."

The food arrives and a tense silence hangs between us as I mow through my fries. I lick the salt off my fingers and stare at my living, breathing father. "Maybe you did make the right choice."

He sets his burger down slowly and looks at me with decades of pain in his eyes.

"Isadora said that everything in my life led me to this point." I chuckle coldly. "I can tell you that my life in Sedona was nothing to brag about. I ran out on three months' back rent and a bunch of other unpaid bills when Silas delivered the money and the will."

"You should pay those bills." He waves the

words away. "Not the point. Please finish what you were saying."

"I don't know what I was saying. All I know is that I'm here. You're here. We're both innocent of murder, and I'm going to prove it."

He smiles broadly and his eyes spill over with pride. "Like I said, there doesn't appear to be any saying 'no' to you."

We share a conspiratorial laugh and finish our burgers.

I turn to wave to Tally and see Odell walking toward the table.

My freshly gobbled burger and fries churn.

My dad grips the edge of the table, and his knuckles whiten as he pushes back into the red vinyl bench seat.

Odell puts up both hands. "I come in peace, Jacob."

My dad relaxes his grip.

I don't care whether he comes in a coat of many colors, I don't like being taken for a ride. "Why didn't you tell me about the fight you had with Cal?"

Odell's gaze snaps to me. "Boy, you don't miss a thing. Not a darn thing."

I purse my lips and stare insistently.

"The truth is always the best defense, kid. I knew it made me look guilty."

"No wonder you were being so nice to me when they threw me in the slammer!"

Jacob leans forward. "What? When?"

I wave him off. "Did you do it?"

Odell's eyes widen and his brow creases. "Murder Cal? You serious, kid?"

"Yes. You have more motive than me. He was trying to take the bookshop, the diner—all your memories of Myrtle. Did you kill him or not?"

"He didn't know about Isadora's will. He assumed she'd been irresponsible, as was her tendency, and thought he'd buy it up 'fore it went on the auction block."

I throw up my hands in frustration. "So?"

"I knew what she'd done—in her will. He was trying to take the bookshop from you, but I couldn't tell him until Silas found you. I'm old, Mitzy. Too old to be slinging burgers in a diner every day. If he was only after the diner, I probably would've taken the money and left town for good. But he was gonna take the bookshop from you."

"But you didn't even know me."

"I knew Myrtle or Isadora, or whatever you wanna call her. I knew how much she regretted never meeting you and how much it meant to her to think that you would get to know her through her bookshop."

Oh, if Odell only knew the half of it.

"I couldn't let him do it." Odell smacks his right fist into his left palm.

"Are you saying you did kill him?" Jacob blurts the accusation and gets to his feet.

"No. No." Odell waves his hands and takes a step back. "I'm saying Myrtle and I rebuilt our relationship when she was ill. I thought if I could keep that bookshop for Mitzy, I could make up for all the ugliness the first time around."

Jacob nods slowly. "My dad could be pretty vindictive."

I look from Odell to Jacob. "Do you believe him, Dad?"

Before Jacob can answer, Odell jumps in. "I'll call Sheriff Harper right now and make a statement if you think it'll make a difference."

I slap my hand on the table. "Since my dad is their latest suspect, I'll take your offer. The more suspects on the list, the better." I point to the phone on the wall behind the counter. "Thanks, Odell. It would mean a lot to Isadora."

Odell hesitates, but he marches over and makes the call.

I pat my dad on the shoulder and we turn to leave.

"Hey, Mitzy," calls Odell.

I glance back.

"My buddy DeVine says that 'bout the only

valid explanation for the absence of rifling on the second bullet woulda been a thing called a sabot."

And that's a Yahtzee for me! A surge of warmth surrounds my heart. "Thanks, Odell."

"Anytime, kid."

Dad and I walk out the door and I turn toward the bookshop.

He pulls away and stands on the sidewalk, chewing the inside of his cheek in an all too familiar way.

"What's up?" I ask.

"This is where we say goodnight, I guess. I'll head back to my hotel and meet you for break—"

"Are you pulling my leg? As far as I'm concerned this day is never going to end. You're coming back to the bookshop and we're having a sleepover."

He laughs. "A sleepover? You sure?"

"Uh, yeah." I look up and down the street. "Where can we get popcorn, Red Vines, ice cream, and possibly pie?"

"Follow me." His arm beckons. "There's a Piggly Wiggly on 4th."

"Is that a store or a livestock barn?"

He laughs so hard he chokes a little.

I pat him on the back and feel happy all over.

CHAPTER 25

Back at the apartment, Dad and I set up camp on the thick Persian rug. He is also sufficiently impressed by the candle handle and the secret phone booth.

I run down to the microwave in the back room and pop two bags of popcorn.

When I return to the apartment, I interrupt a standoff between Pyewacket and Dad.

"Is that thing yours?" asks Dad.

"That is Pyewacket. Grams said he's a caracal. He was her rescue and he's spoiled rotten." I toss a hot bag of popcorn to Jacob and turn my attention to the furry beast. "Pye, Dad's cool. If you don't back down, I will 'forget' to give you Fruity Puffs in the morning."

Pyewacket shakes his hackles down, twitches

his ear tufts, and yawns.

Dad looks at me. "That can't be the original Pyewacket? But does he talk, too?"

"What?" I chuckle and shake my head.

"Hey, your ghost grandmother haunts this place and apparently communicates with you. Why would it be so strange if that wildcat talked?"

"You got me there." I shrug. "I have no idea if he's 'original' or not. And if he talks, he doesn't talk to me, but he seems to understand when I talk to him." I toss a piece of popped corn toward Pye. His powerful hind legs propel him through the air and he snatches the fluffy white projectile with ease.

"I'd hate to be a sparrow in his line of sight."

"Or an eyeball," I mumble.

"What's that?" Dad leans on the stack of pillows under his arm.

I quickly explain how Cal was discovered in the alley behind the bookshop. I skim over the gory details of Pye's involvement. I need several Red Vines to calm my stomach.

"What was Cal doing in the alley?"

"Oh, he definitely wasn't killed in the alley. The ME at county confirmed that he was killed somewhere else. The body was frozen to obscure time of death." I shiver.

"Someone was definitely trying to set you up."

Jacob sits up and crunches absently on a handful of popcorn.

"Me? Why would they want to set me up? No one in this town even knows me."

"But they know me."

"Huh?" Pyewacket rubs against me and I scratch between his ears. "So were they framing you?"

"All I know is that I wasn't having an affair with Kitty, and I had no idea that Cal was changing his will. One set of facts makes me look guilty and the other points toward innocence." He munches on another handful of popcorn.

I reach for my bag and discover Pye's head shoved so far into the bag that his tufts are all that's showing. "Pye! You little thief!" I swat at his tan backside.

He shakes the bag off and popcorn flies everywhere.

Jacob laughs so hard his eyes water.

I want to be furious, but the sound of my dad's laughter warms my heart. I chuckle and start to collect the scattered kernels.

"Here, let me help." He grabs a trash can and picks up a handful.

I wave my hands. "Hey, don't throw it away! I plan on eating that." I pass him the popcorn bag.

"Put 'em back in here. I'm not terribly fussy when it comes to my snack foods."

We get the mess under control just as Grams makes an appearance.

She clutches her pearls and dabs at her eyes. "I never thought I'd see this day! Dear, do you think Jacob would like to look at some photo albums?" She swirls nervously above my dad.

"That sounds wonderful, Grams."

Jacob stiffens and his eyes dart left and right. "She's here? Now? Is she by me?"

I laugh a little. "Sorry, Dad. I'm so used to her popping in and out now, I forget to announce her entrances." I point to a spot above and to the left. "She's right there."

He looks over his shoulder and smiles. "Hey, Mom."

She rushes toward him and he shivers.

"I felt something cold. Is that her?" His skin is peppered with goosebumps.

"That's her." I look at my own arms and shrug. "I don't get the chills from her. Never did. I saw her right away, and we could talk. Maybe it's because I can see her?"

"I'm sure that's it, dear." Grams nods her head and floats away from my shivering dad. "Ask him about the albums."

"Oh, right. Grams asked if you'd like to look at photo albums?"

"That sounds great."

"Over here, honey." Grams swooshes over to a built-in bookcase and gestures to a row of volumes.

I grab a couple and return to the floor next to my dad.

The first album is ancient. The pages are black construction paper with tiny red paper corners stuck to the pages. Each black-and-white photo is tucked snuggly into a group of four corner-holders.

Jacob runs his fingers along the page. "I think this is Cal as a baby, but I don't recognize anyone else."

Grams swirls closer.

The hair on my dad's arm stands up.

"Those are Cal's grandparents. And that boy pulling the wagon is Cal's older brother. He was killed in Vietnam." Grams sniffles.

I touch the image of the young boy. "How sad."

Dad looks at me. "What's sad?"

Oh, right. I'm the only one who can hear the ghost. I repeat the story about Cal's older brother.

Jacob touches the picture and shakes his head. "He never talked about it, but it definitely explains his obsession with making the family railroad successful."

We work our way through the album, Grams

giving me the stories and me sharing them with my dad. It's a strange and emotional history lesson.

As the snacks run low and my eyelids grow heavy, I close the fourth album. "I'm beat, Dad. Mind if I grab a few before the sun comes up?"

"Sure," he says. His voice sounds sad.

"Is everything all right?"

He takes my hand in his large strong one and squeezes gently. "I guess part of me is afraid that if I close my eyes, you'll be gone when I open them up. Dreams like this are what kept me sane all those years in prison, but I never thought for a minute it could be real."

I throw my arms around him. "It's real. I'm not an orphan and you're not in prison. It's real, and tomorrow we're going to show this town what happens when you cross the Duncans."

"And Mitzy Moon," says Dad with a chuckle.

CHAPTER 26

AFTER A PERFECT BREAKFAST at the diner, Jacob and I walk down to the sheriff's station.

The waiting area is nearly empty. Apparently the weekday Pin Cherry Festival activities aren't as well attended as opening weekend.

A swarthy little man with a messy black mustache, five-o-clock shadow at nine in the morning, and a paunch hanging way over his belt, catches my eye.

"You Jackson?"

He looks up. "Who wants to know?"

I smile and cross my arms. "Seems like the conversation isn't over after all."

Jackson scowls at me and leans forward.

I don't like the way he's looking at me.

My dad steps up and adds his prison-tough presence to my side.

Jackson's eyes widen. "You're the son. Jacob Duncan."

I'm not sure if it's a good or bad thing that he recognizes my dad.

"Why did my grandfather hire you?" I ask, hoping to catch him off balance.

The pint-sized PI looks around nervously. "It's not safe. I'm telling you right now, leave it alone."

My dad leans down and growls, "Are you threatening my little girl?"

I never felt so happy to be called a little girl in my entire life.

"It's not me you need to worry about."

"Mr. Jackson, the sheriff will see you now," the Furious-Monkeys-playing clerk announces.

Sheriff Erick takes one look at me and strides into the waiting area. "Moon, I told you to let this go. Leave the investigation to the professionals."

"Oh, is that what you're calling this circus act?" That was so much harsher than I intended. Too late. "If it wasn't for my amateur investigation you never would've found this guy." I point to Jackson and narrow my gaze. "And by the looks of him he's hiding something."

Sheriff Erick steps closer to me.

My skin tingles.

"I'm warning you, Moon."

"Oh, everyone is full of warnings today." I wave it away with a flick of my wrist. "I'll have Silas pick up a copy of Jackson's statement this afternoon."

I hook my arm through my dad's elbow and walk toward the door. I throw one last comment over my shoulder. "And, you're welcome."

Dad heads off to meet with Cal's attorney to see if he can get to the bottom of the will-changing rumor and I wander back to the bookshop.

I learn from the empty establishment and a close inspection of the sign in the window that we're closed on Mondays. I walk upstairs and plunk down next to the file boxes.

Things are still a mess from the sleepover, so I go through my stacks and organize the reports and other documents as I pack the lot back into the cardboard containers. I'll see if Twiggy wants to return them tomorrow.

My hands linger on the security guard's statement. Something is off. Why is he the only witness who claims to have heard the third shot?

Grams drifts down next to me with a pleading look on her face and an overall "depleted" appearance.

"What is it? What's going on?"

She flashes back to technicolor. "I know you didn't say it out loud, dear, but why don't you see if you can track that guard down and ask him yourself?"

I channel Kitty for a second. "Brilliant!"

I brush my teeth, and apply an extra layer of flirty mascara to make my eyelashes pop and some fresh lip tint.

"That should do the trick." Grams winks. "What man could say 'no' to that face?"

"Sheriff Erick, for one," I reply bitterly.

"Oh don't you fret. He'll come around."

"Wish me luck." I grab the keys to the Mercedes and head off toward the larger town to the north, Broken Rock. That town was desperate for the tax revenues and allowed the big box store that Pin Cherry Harbor had refused.

The address on the coffee-stained witness statement is over fifteen years old, but I have to start somewhere.

The drive through Black Cap Trail and Pancake Bay, along the coast of the magnificently massive body of fresh water, loosens some of the knots in my neck.

Most of the bravado I throw down in front of Sheriff Erick is for show. Deep down I'm still a little terrified that my dad or I could wind up taking the rap for Cal's murder.

Near the outskirts of Broken Rock, I speak the address into the map app on my phone. I paid off my past due bill and the exorbitant re-activation fee, but at least I have a phone now.

Look at me, "adulting" like an— Well, you get the idea.

"You have arrived at your destination," announces the helpful phone.

I check the house number against the old police report. Yep, I have arrived.

I scope my makeup in the rearview mirror and press my lips together to even out the color. All right, let's go get the truth.

I open the small gate, close it quietly behind, and make my way up the old, buckled sidewalk. As I mount the steps to the porch, I notice the front door is ajar.

The hairs on the back of my neck jump to attention. This is the part in the movie when the star grabs their gun.

I don't have a gun.

I'm probably seriously overreacting. Maybe the man just didn't latch his door. Maybe I've actually seen too many movies.

There's no stack of decaying newspapers piled up on the porch so it's safe to assume someone who lives in the house has passed through this door in the last twenty-four hours. I recite this invented factoid to calm my frayed nerves.

I ring the doorbell several times. This way if the

guy is home he'll absolutely hear, and if there's an intruder inside, they'll have ample warning and hopefully bolt out the back door.

No one answers.

No one bolts.

It's deadly quiet. Why did I say that?

I push open the solid wooden door and it creaks with appropriate Scooby Doo intensity.

Nice and loud, I shout, "Delivery for Mr. Whitakker. Anyone here?"

Nada. Bupkus.

The plain white blinds in the living room and the complete lack of throw pillows on the lumpy sofa lead me to believe Mr. Whitakker lives alone.

I give one more shout, "Hello? Is any—?"

My throat tightens and cuts off my voice. I freeze with one foot on the stained grey linoleum and one foot on the threadbare brown carpet. There are other feet.

These feet are not standing feet. They're covered by the soles of a man's slippers, and I'm afraid to report that they seem to be attached to a body.

I put my hand over my mouth to capture the inevitable scream.

I step into the kitchen and lean around the cabinet.

I scream into my hand and search the room.

I've never been so grateful for cell service in my

entire life. I run out of the death house, leave the door open, and I dial as I run. Please don't be on a coffee break, Furious Monkeys!

She answers. "Pin Cherry Sheriff's Station. How may I direct your call?"

"I need Sheriff Erick—Harper, right away. It's an emergency." My breath comes in little gasps.

"You should have called 911 if—"

"Put Erick on the line. I've got a dead body here!" Okay, maybe I lost it a little. But I don't "do" dead bodies.

"Sheriff Harper here."

"Erick, it's Mitzy. He's dead. I came to ask him some questions, and the door was open and then a body—there's so much—I mean, it's fresh—"

"Miss Moon? Where are you?"

I recite the address.

"What are you doing in Broken Rock?"

"I wanted to question the security guard. Something just didn't sit right with me—"

"Miss Moon, I need you to get in your car and drive directly back to this station. Can you do that?"

"But the body, and I wanted to know about the third shot—"

"Mitzy, this is serious. There was no third shot. The security guard was the inside guy."

"What? That doesn't make any sense. Does my dad know about this?"

"Mitzy, please get out of that house."

I'm temporarily distracted by the desperate concern in Erick's voice, so I don't let him know that I'm already in my car.

"If you come to the station, I'll let you read Jackson's statement."

I know it's a blatant bribe but— "Deal."

I lock myself inside the Mercedes and drive as fast as my heart is racing. I figure a dead body is the best excuse I'll ever have for speeding.

CHAPTER 27

I RUSH INTO the sheriff's station and am surprised to see my dad in the waiting area. He's lounging in a chair, absently rubbing the sleeve of his light-blue Oxford shirt between his thumb and forefinger.

He looks up and smiles. "Harper asked me to come back in."

"Did he say why?"

"Something to do with the PI's statement. I asked Silas to meet me here, just in case."

Oh boy. This does not sound good. As much as I believe in my dad's innocence, I'm growing increasingly concerned about this private investigator's involvement. What if he killed the security guard? I cross my arms and pinch myself. Get it together, Moon.

Sheriff Harper walks out of his office and looks

from me to my dad. "Good, you're both here. I'll need you to come to my office."

I didn't hear the word arrest. I follow without formal protest.

Jacob is the first to speak. "What's all this about, Harper? What was that PI up to?"

Erick closes his door and motions for us to take the seats in front of his desk.

My nerves are shot and I don't have it in me to argue. I collapse into a stiff brown chair.

Erick shuffles some papers on his desk and sighs. "Cal hired the PI to look into your old case, Jacob."

"My case? Why?"

"I don't think we'll ever know for sure, but Mr. Jackson was paid for one thing and one thing only: to find out what actually happened the night of the robbery." Erick moves the same papers around again.

I lean forward and put both hands on the edge of his metal-topped desk. "And?"

"I have to follow a couple leads and verify some of the information—"

"But?" I strum my fingers impatiently.

"But it sounds like Jackson found some evidence that would refute Darrin's testimony."

My father leans back in his chair. The wood

creaks as he squares his shoulders and clenches his jaw. "What kind of evidence?"

"Jackson spoke to the security guard. He had a deal with Darrin to destroy the monitoring equipment and the tape from the day of the robbery. Darrin was supposed to cut him in on thirty percent of the take."

"News to me," my dad grumbles through gritted teeth.

Erick nods and continues, "When Darrin got caught the guard threatened to come forward, but Darrin promised Whitakker an extra $10,000 to keep quiet."

My dad's hands grip his knees, and the only sound in the room is his fingers squeezing across the denim fabric. "Darrin didn't have that kind of money," he growls.

"Not all the stolen cash was recovered. It seems like Darrin had time to stash some of it somewhere and he used it to bribe the guard. He promised him more when he got out." Erick drops the papers on his desk and leans back in his chair. "He made the deal with the district attorney to make sure he got out before you."

"Worked out pretty well for good ol' Darrin. He was sentenced to forty-eight months and got out in thirty-two with time off for good behavior."

I put my hand on top of my dad's tense fingers. "I'm so sorry, Dad."

He shakes off my sympathy.

I sigh and continue questioning Erick. "Who killed Whitakker?" I shudder as the image from the kitchen floor in Broken Rock looms in my memory.

Sheriff Erick sighs. "Jackson claims Whitakker kept the security footage as insurance, and for blackmail. As long as Darrin kept the payments trickling in, the tape was safe. Of course, once Jackson found out about the tape, Cal offered a massive payoff to get his hands on it. Someone wanted to make sure that didn't happen."

My dad's white knuckles crack and his teeth grind. "Darrin."

"That's what we're thinking too." Erick leans back and shakes his head sadly.

I look from Erick to my dad and back. "So, Darrin killed Whitakker."

Jacob's voice cracks as he adds, "And Cal."

"And Cal," I whisper. The wind goes out of my sails. My witty banter vanishes. "What now?"

"We have a statewide BOLO out on Darrin MacIntyre, but something tells me he hasn't left the area." Erick locks eyes with my dad. "What do you think, Jacob?"

"He's gonna finish what he started."

"We'd like to put you in protective custody."

238 / TRIXIE SILVERTALE

Jacob reaches for my hand. "Both of us?"

"We have no reason to believe Mitzy's in danger."

Jacob stands and the room seems to shrink to half its size. "He dumped a body in the alley behind her bookshop and she just walked out of a murder scene. I'm not leaving her unprotected."

"I understand your concern, Jacob. We're a small force. We feel you're the target. It's unlikely that Darrin is even aware of Mitzy's presence in Pin Cherry, or her connection to you."

My dad's fists ball up tightly.

I jump up and step between them. "Why don't you just stay with me, Dad? We'll have a sleepover, and I'm sure Sheriff Harper can spare a patrol car to keep an eye on the bookshop." I look at Erick with a desperation I can't hide. "Deal?"

He nods. "I can arrange that. We'll find him. Don't worry."

"I hope you find him before I do." Jacob puts a hand on the sheriff's desk and leans down. "I don't mind making good on that murder charge."

I grab my dad's arm and pull him out of the station before he says— Well, it's too late for that, but I don't want Erick to lock him up.

We walk silently back to my car.

"Take me out to Cal's place."

"I don't think we want to stir things up with Kitty. Let's—" My voice cracks as I plead.

"I need to pick something up." He stares straight ahead and his jaw is set.

I don't like the look in his eye or the last thing he said to Erick. "Dad, I don't want you to get a gun. Please don't do what you're thinking."

"Darrin needs to pay for everything he took from me."

I can't stop them. The waterworks burst. "But he could take so much more. Please, Dad, I'm begging you. I just found you. Don't let this revenge take you away from me again."

His eyes soften and he looks at me. "He killed my father, Mitzy."

"And now you want to give him a chance to kill mine?" I sob uncontrollably.

He scoops me into his arms and his chest heaves as he chokes back his own emotion. "All right, you win. Let's have that sleepover."

CHAPTER 28

THE FESTIVE MOOD of our previous sleepover is absent as we walk into the darkened bookshop. I press the flashlight app on my phone and we walk somberly toward the staircase.

The uplifting feeling of bonding has evaporated and the heavy weight of Darrin's betrayal hangs over us like a dark storm cloud.

I unhook the "No Admittance" chain, and Jacob and I circle up the metal staircase.

In the apartment, we straighten pillows and blankets in silence. I can't stand it.

"Dad?"

The eyes that look over at me are dark and empty.

"I can't imagine what you must be feeling right now, but—"

He lifts a hand to stop me. "Darrin was my friend. It's not about the money or the side-deal with the security guard. That was classic Darrin. He always hedged his bets. That slippery side-deal crap is what got him tossed out of the Navy." Dad folds a pillow and punches his large fist into the feathers. "He stole fifteen years of my life."

I nod. "And he stole you away from me." I sit down on the floor and rest my small hand on top of my dad's fist. "But the truth has finally come out. We're together, and the police can take care of Darrin."

He sighs. "I hear what you're saying, Mitzy. My brain agrees, but my broken heart wants revenge. I need to make Darrin pay."

The veins in Jacob's arm pop up as his fist tightens.

I pull away—helpless.

He jumps as goosebumps cover his skin.

"Grams?" I look up.

"Sounds like a good news/bad news situation, dear. What happened?"

I bring her up to speed on the security guard, and Darrin's killing spree.

"Poor Cal. He was trying to make things right with Jacob. He wanted another chance." She floats toward the coffered ceiling. "Poor, poor Cal."

Desperate to shift the mood, I lift up the remaining packet of microwave popcorn and say, "Wanna split this?"

Jacob pulls his mind back from whatever road it had traveled down and smiles. "Sounds good." He snags the pack from my hand and stands. "Microwave is in the back room, right?"

"Correct. Two minutes and twenty seconds should do it."

He chuckles. "Give or take, eh?"

I blush and nod. I'll spare him the story of the burned popcorn, the smoke alarm, and the horrible scent that still lingers in the back room.

Jacob leaves and I turn to Grams. "Can you believe this Darrin jerk? I mean, how did Dad even end up being friends with such a colossal—"

Grams interrupts my tirade. "They were best buddies since sixth grade, or thereabouts. Darrin's family moved into town and the boys hit it off. They played football together. Cal would take them hunting, and they were inseparable."

"But Darrin is evil!" I stand and pace to the window.

"He was always the instigator, but in high school it was fairly harmless things like staying out past curfew and stealing a few beers from the fridge. Darrin didn't go completely off the rails until he got expelled from school."

"College?"

"He never made it. He was caught stealing some test answers their senior year and the school had a zero-tolerance policy. He was expelled." Grams floats toward me.

I chew on a Red Vine and nod my head. "He never got his GED or anything?"

"I can't say for sure, dear. But Darrin was furious about the injustice. Your dad went off to college and Darrin joined the Navy for a spell, but he was dishonorably discharged in no time. Once he was back on the street, he couldn't let go."

I plop down on the settee and reach for another Red Vine. "What do you mean?"

"Simply, that Darrin hounded your father endlessly. He would take him out every weekend, and eventually every night. Your dad always liked to party, so it didn't take much pressure to get him to ignore his studies."

I could relate to the aimless party cycle. "Did Dad drop out or get kicked out?"

"His grades plummeted. Cal cut off his allowance and threatened to stop paying for college. Jacob loved to rail against authority." She turns away and I assume she's hiding her tears.

"But how did they go from partying to robbery?" I ask.

Grams goes absolutely still. It is strange. It looks like when you press pause on a movie.

"What is it?"

She flickers. "How long has Jacob been gone, dear?"

I shrug.

She vanishes through the wall and comes flying back a few seconds later, like a ghost comet.

"He's here!"

I don't have to ask "who." The fear on her face tells me everything.

I grab my phone to call Erick. It's DEAD! I must've left the stupid flashlight app on.

"The phone booth," says Grams.

I run to the corner and push the wall. The door pops open and I pick up the receiver. "The line is dead," I shout. I have to stop saying that word.

"You've got to go for help, Mitzy." Grams is a fright. She's fading in and out like a signal that's not quite strong enough.

I nod and smile. "Wish me luck."

"Take Pye. He can create a distraction."

Sure, why not place my life in the paws of a psycho-cat.

I open the bookcase door. Pyewacket races past me.

I creep toward the spiral staircase. I don't smell burnt popcorn, so I assume Jacob never made it to the back room.

Pyewacket's low menacing growl chills my

blood.

Before I can shush the cat, the scrape of a metal door slowly opening and closing interrupts. I close my eyes and replay the sound. I remember hearing the click of a push bar before the scrape, not the twist of a handle. They went into the museum.

I hurry down the stairs and feel my way along the stacks toward the "Employees Only" door. There's no time to go for help. It's me or nothing.

I don't know what's on the other side of that door, but if there's any chance I can save my father . . . I depress the push bar as quietly as possible and apply slow steady pressure to the door.

So far so good. The door barely makes a sound.

A furry creature brushes past my leg and through the narrow opening.

I clamp my jaw shut and scream silently. That demon-spawn!

I take a slow breath in through my nose and listen for any clue as to Darrin and Jacob's location.

Grams pops up next to me and sends my heart into a bucking bronco routine. I don't have to worry about Darrin getting his hands on me; Grams and Pye will kill me long before he discovers me.

"Don't even joke about such a thing, Mitzy!"

Oh right, she can hear my thoughts. I'll let it slide for now. *All right, Grams, I'm allowing telepathic communication. Where are they?*

She vanishes from my side.

The crashes, thunks, and groans would indicate a struggle. A couple of thuds. Another groan.

Grams reappears. "He's forcing your father up to the roof. I don't like this one bit."

Neither do I.

"Follow me." Grams swooshes across the floor.

I hurry along and— "Mm— Gr—" I clap one hand over my mouth and press on my bruised hip with the other. *I can't walk through Gutenberg presses, Grams.*

"I'm so sorry, dear. I was worried about Jacob and I forgot about— Never mind. Hurry, Mitzy."

I rub my bone bruise once more and follow her to the back stairs.

The struggle is growing more violent. *They're way ahead of me. Grams, can't you do something? I'll never get there in time.*

"What can I do, honey? I can't talk to your dad and I've tried to move things, but I'm no Patrick Swayze."

There has to be something, Grams. You're made of some kind of energy. I can see you. Pyewacket can sense you—

Where's Pye?

Grams flies up the stairwell.

I creep up as quickly as I can without making a racket.

"Ree-ooow!"

CRASH!

"Son of a—"

I don't recognize that voice. It must be Darrin. Good job, Pye. Extra Fruity Puffs for you!

I rush up the steps.

The sick wallop of fists connecting with flesh echoes down the stairwell.

The thud, thud, thud of a body falling down the steps.

I cross the landing and the body crashes into my leg.

Oh dear Lord, please let that be Jacob.

"Dad?" I whisper.

"Mitzy, get out of here. This is my fight."

I grab his arm and help him to his feet. "Come on, Dad."

"What a special moment." A harsh laugh echoes down the stairwell. "Nobody's going anywhere. Isn't that right, Jake?"

I look up and see the outline of a gun barrel illuminated in the dim stairwell—pointing straight down the stairs. Straight at my head.

"You know what, Jake? I came back to make sure you went back to prison for life, but imagine my surprise when I discovered your long lost baby girl. How about I kill her first—"

"You'll never get away with this, Darrin." I'm

just spitballing now, but this is the point in every movie when the good guy gets the bad guy to talk.

"But I already got away with it." Darrin points the gun at my dad as he taunts me. "Maybe I'll kill him first. Cops are already looking at you for Cal's murder, princess. If you kill Jake too, that oughta convince 'em."

"They know about the sabot, Darrin." I can barely make out his face in the darkness, but the lack of a snappy comeback leads me to believe this is news to him. "And they recovered the tape from Whitakker's place."

His deep, satisfied laugh fills the museum.

My mouth goes dry and my throat feels like it's closing.

"You shoulda quit while you were ahead, girlie." He walks down another step closer to us. "You torpedoed your own lifeboat."

Jacob pushes me behind his tree trunk of a body.

"I made sure ol' Whit told me the location of the tape before I killed him."

I shiver uncontrollably. I mean, I was pretty sure Darrin killed the security guard, but hearing him brag about murdering someone makes me a little sick to my stomach.

"Once I take care of you and your patsy of a daddy, I'll take this handy key" —he jingles a key ring— "and pick up the tape from Whit's safe deposit box. The last bit of evidence that can clear your pops will be gone. He'll die a murderer."

He steps down. "And you'll be that pathetic millennial that committed murder but then got so 'emo' that she offed herself."

"Let her go, Darrin. Your beef is with me."

"Always the hero." Darrin spits on the stairs. "Why do you think I set you up, buddy? Because I knew you were too stupid to figure it out and too weak to fight back."

The museum lights start flashing like a disco.

You go Grams! If that's you . . .

"Prison changes people." Dad shoves me down toward the ground and lunges at Darrin.

"No!" I scream.

Everything flashes before my eyes like a stop-action movie.

The pulsing lights show me bits and pieces.

The gun fires.

Fur flies.

"Reeee-OW!"

Pyewacket's furry form falls slack on the stairs.

Jacob has one arm around Darrin's neck, slowly choking the life out of him, while the other hand struggles to control the gun.

Another bullet fires, narrowly missing my head and embedding in the brick.

The lights stop flickering and stay on.

The welcome sound of heavy-soled boots running across the concrete museum floor races toward me.

"Up here," I scream.

Darrin and my dad tumble down the stairs past the still-unmoving Pye.

Sheriff Erick lunges up the stairs two at a time and pushes me out of the way just as the wrestling duo hits the landing.

"Freeze!"

My dad comes up with the gun and aims it at Darrin's head.

"Dad, no." I'm shaking uncontrollably. "Please, Daddy. Please don't do it." I can't stop the tears.

"Go ahead, Jake. Pull the trigger." Darrin's words are filled with the bravado of a man who knows his life is a heartbeat from ending.

Sheriff Erick moves his aim from Darrin to my dad. "Jacob, drop the gun. Let us handle this now. Don't do something you'll regret."

Deputy Paulsen shoves past me to even things up. "Don't move, scumbag."

I can't believe she's aiming at my dad too! And still pulling cheesy one-liners from eighties cop movies! I wipe my tears and prepare to tackle her.

"Come on, Jake. You know you want to end this

once and for all." Darrin baits my dad. "You know you need to settle this score."

"You might be able to frame me for murder, Darrin, but you can't actually turn me into a killer." Jacob spins the gun around and hands it to Sheriff Erick, grip first.

Darrin lunges up.

My dad's knee connects with Darrin's face in a bone-splintering crunch.

Darrin cradles his face with both hands. "My nose! He broke my nose!"

Grams appears. "Good job! That's my boy!"

"Step away, Jacob." Erick nods his head toward me. "Both of you, clear out." He moves closer to Darrin. "Darrin MacIntyre, you're under arrest for the murders . . . "

Murders. Plural. That's all I need to hear. I smile through my tears and shove past Deputy Paulsen to hug my dad.

Erick and Deputy Paulsen cuff Darrin and drag him off, to the cheers of my Ghost-ma.

"He's got a key to Whitakker's safe deposit box. Make sure you get that!" I shout to the departing law-enforcement duo.

I squeeze my dad once more, drop my arms, and slowly approach Pyewacket's twisted shape.

I reach out my shaky, grateful hand to touch his brave, motionless body. And I pass out.

CHAPTER 29

Bright sunlight warms my cheek and I stretch my arms. As I luxuriate on the soft mattress beneath me with the cozy comforter over me, for a split second, I believe it was all a horrible dream.

But the image of precious Pyewacket on that staircase—

I sit up and look for my dad. "Grams! Grams! Where is everyone?"

She fades in right next to me and I jump.

"Your phone is fully charged and it's on the bedside table. Silas said to call him as soon as you got out of bed."

"Where's my dad? Did they arrest him?"

"No, dear. Bless his heart. He came in and whispered to these four walls that he was going down to the station to view the tape. I'm sure that was for my benefit, but that was hours ago."

How could I have slept so late? I grab my phone and press. It's after noon. I've been asleep forever.

"You were scared out of your wits, honey. You needed a good—"

I point to my lips. "The crisis has passed, Grams. Standing rules apply."

"Of course."

I call Silas.

"Good afternoon, Mitzy. How are you feeling?"

"Who cares about me? Where's Pye? Can I see the body before he's laid to rest? Is there a pet cemetery in Pin Cherry? We should have a service. Maybe the sheriff will give him some kind of medal."

I do not appreciate my attorney's hearty laugh.

"Actually, Mitzy, we all care about you a great deal. And I'm afraid Pye did take a bullet for you and Jacob."

My eyes well up. I never should've called him a demon spawn. "He's dead? That poor, sweet kitten."

"Not exactly. Robin Pyewacket Goodfellow has certainly given one of his lives, but it appears it was not his ninth. He's heavily sedated at the Pin Cherry Harbor Animal Hospital. You may visit him anytime."

I can't help but cry. That irritating furry fiend saved my stupid life. I sniffle loudly and continue, "What about my dad? Where's he?"

"It would seem that VHS tape players are not as plentiful as they once were. Sheriff Erick has requested one be brought up from the big city. However, Twiggy heard about the dilemma and claims she can acquire one, post haste. Your father and I are enjoying a late repast at the diner and awaiting the arrival of the required tech."

I hang up without replying.

I look down at yesterday's skinny jeans and cashmere sweater. I don't know where the blood came from but it's oogy and I want it off me. I search through the pile of clothes on the floor of the closet and find an acceptably clean pair of jeans. I pull them on and shove my finger in to tuck the pockets down.

I pull out the black button gift from Pyewacket. I turn it over in my hands. And I suddenly know exactly where this button came from—

"Navy peacoat!"

Grams swooshes down. "Where did you get that?"

"The amazing Pye brought it in from the alley. I'll bet you Twiggy's next paycheck that this is a button from Darrin's coat."

"You better give that to the sheriff."

"Right after breakfast. I don't think I can see him on an empty stomach."

"Honestly, Mitzy." Grams rolls her ghost eyes.

I shrug and pull on my boots as I hop through the secret door.

I run down the spiral steps two at a time and . . . flip over the chain at full speed. "Twiggy!"

There's no reply.

Grams hovers next to me. "She came in early, but then she had to run off to get the tape player thingy."

Curses. I check my face for gum or other floor souvenirs and resume my rapid run—now it's more of a limp—to Myrtle's Diner.

I push open the door of the diner. There's my dad—alive and well. The scent of golden, delicious french fries envelopes me. This is my idea of heaven.

My dad is out of the booth before I can take another step. We meet in the middle and hug like we haven't seen each other in twenty-one years.

Tally claps and sniffles.

"Breakfast or lunch?" Odell calls from the back.

I'm pretty sure that's not onions making his eyes water. Boy, I'll never get used to how fast news travels in a small town. "Both," I say with enthusiasm.

Dad puts his arm around my shoulder and we slide into the booth across the table from Silas.

"Any news on Darrin?" I ask as I blindly reach for the steaming mug of coffee Tally set on the table.

"Nothing official, but I believe it would not be premature to say that Darrin MacIntyre will never again experience life outside of a prison cell." Silas nods appreciatively and takes a sip of his coffee.

"As it should be," growls Jacob.

I lift my mug and get a nose full of whipped cream. I pull back and look down in confusion.

Tally smiles from across the restaurant and says, "Half coffee, half hot chocolate, topped with fresh whip. I thought you could use a little pampering."

I smile gratefully as I wipe the whip off my nose and come at the delicious smelling beverage from another angle. After I manage a couple sips, I give a big "thumbs up" to Tally. "Perfection."

She giggles and scurries to the orders-up window.

The rest of our wonderful, celebratory meal is spent discussing who was more awesome in our fight for our lives against Darrin.

As I lick the salt off my fingers, I say, "Obviously, the award goes to Pyewacket, hands down."

"Hands down," Jacob and Silas say in unison.

There's a beep, and Silas pulls his phone out of the pocket of his wrinkled brown suit.

I stare at the cell phone and smirk at my own private joke. For some reason I expected Silas to have a miniature rotary phone in his pocket, or maybe a Morse code thingy.

"Text from Sheriff Harper. Looks like they're ready for us." He slips the phone back in his pocket and slides out of the booth.

Jacob drops several crumpled bills on the table, and Silas lays a crisp twenty next to the pile.

We walk down to the station in anticipatory silence.

Jacob holds the door for Silas and me.

Sheriff Erick waits for us in the—area designated for such a purpose.

"Good afternoon," he says.

"Hey Erick." I grin.

His cheeks flush, but I can't tell if it's from irritation or embarrassment.

"How's Darrin's face?" I couldn't care less about that jerk's broken nose, but I enjoy bringing it up immensely.

Erick shakes his head. "He'll live."

"That's a shame," I retort.

"A real shame," echoes my dad.

The television and VHS player are set up in the station's small conference room.

I look around at the bland wood paneling and the chipped veneer on the table. I bet this room has seen some things. More than its share of donuts at the very least!

Jacob pulls out a faded blue chair for me and we settle in to watch the day his life turned to—crap.

Sheriff Erick dims the lights. "There's no audio."

We stare at the wiggly screen.

"Give it a second for the tracking to adjust," says Erick.

Whatever you say. Like I know anything about tracking.

The image stabilizes and I can see it's a small office. Nothing stands out in the black-and-white image.

The door, which is at the top of our screen, blasts open and a scared little man with thick glasses walks in with his hands up.

The dashing Darrin has a gun shoved in the guy's back.

My dad shifts in his seat.

A young, handsome Jacob is next to appear in the pantomime on the screen. The guy in glasses points up at the camera and my dad aims—

The screen goes black.

My dad's shoulders slump. Silas turns to shake his head in our direction.

"There's more," says the sheriff.

The screen comes to life again with footage from a completely different angle. Looks like the store manager wasn't as stupid as Darrin assumed. And the security guard must've planned to black-mail him all along.

The new angle seems to be from a camera on the desk across from the safe.

Darrin shoves the manager down on the ground and holds the gun to the back of his head.

The manager shakes violently with fear.

We can't see the safe open, but we see zippered bank bags being handed up to Darrin.

The bags stop.

Darrin roughs up the manager, shoves him to the side, and looks into the safe.

Suddenly a large hand appears at the bottom of the screen.

It's hard to tell, but from this perspective it looks as though the manager might be reaching for the phone.

Darrin grabs something and the manager gets flung up against the safe.

"Close your eyes." There's no emotion in my dad's words.

I close them immediately.

Next to me, my dad flinches.

"Despicable," murmurs Silas.

"That tape and the evidence we found at Darrin's place will be more than enough to clear you of the murder charge, Jacob."

"Oh, and this." I take the black button bearing the fouled anchor from my pocket and set it on the table. "Pye brought it in from the alley. I swear I wasn't poking around. I didn't even know what it was until my dad mentioned Darrin's dishonorable discharge from the Navy."

Sheriff Erick looks at the button, picks it up, and shakes his head. "I'm not sure if you're lucky, talented, or diabolical."

"Can I be all three?" I smile as innocently as I know how.

My father interrupts our mutual admiration society. "You were saying—about the murder charge?"

Sheriff Harper nods and continues, "The conviction will be expunged from your record."

I turn to hug my dad, but I'm not prepared for the look on his face.

His eyes are red and his jaw is clenched tight.

I swallow hard. I don't know what to say. I can't begin to imagine how hard that must've been for him to watch. "I'm sorry you had to see that, Dad."

"That poor man. Why did he reach for that phone?" Dad slams his fist on the wobbly table. "Darrin was always overreacting."

Silas stands and places a firm hand on my dad's

shoulder. "It's in the past, Jacob. Your anger won't bring that man back."

I watch as my father's shoulders relax and his breathing calms.

I force a smile to my face. "Let's go see if Pyewacket needs some Fruity Puffs."

Jacob nods and follows me out of the station.

"I have no idea where the animal hospital is. Do you?"

Jacob looks down at me and a faraway mist fills his gaze. "I went there once with Cal. He hit a dog out on some back road. I can probably find it."

I fish the Mercedes keys out of my pocket. "My car's parked back by the bookshop."

"Don't tell your Grams you let me drive it." He chuckles as he takes the keys.

"Why not?"

"It was one of the many things that Isadora 'strictly forbade' when I was growing up." He spins the key chain around his finger. "The Mercedes."

I'm not sure I like the way he says that. I'm already hoping I won't regret this.

We arrive at the animal hospital in one piece. However, I'm going to enact Isadora's rules for all future car rides. My dad is what you'd call a "lead foot" and I'm sure he purposely took the longest route possible to the vet.

I take a couple deep breaths to settle my stomach and pop open the gull-wing door.

Dad walks around and offers me a hand. His face-splitting grin unnerves me.

I snatch the keys from his hand. "I'll be driving back."

For a moment he looks like an over-eager puppy. "Are you sure?"

"Positive." I walk into the stark white clinic and approach the über-modern reception desk.

A man with Tally's smile and Tilly's pouf of grey hair jumps to his feet. "Mitzy Moon, as I live and breathe!" He extends a hand.

I roll the dice. "Ledo?"

"Well now, they said you were sharp as a tack!" He grabs my hand and nearly shakes my arm off. "I bet you're here to see that brave kitty."

"Looks like I'm not the only one getting top marks today, Ledo."

Tally's brother's confusion transforms into amusement before my eyes. He swats me on the back and guffaws. "And sassy as a cucumber, too!"

Don't look at me. I had no idea vegetables could be sassy.

Ledo opens the door to a small recovery room. "The bullet grazed his scapula and punctured his lung—but the good news is that it missed the liver."

He sweeps his arm forward and smiles sympathetically. "You can stay as long as you like."

I whisper my thanks as I walk past and enter.

The sight of the large and powerful Pyewacket lying motionless on a tiny bed with tubes coming out of him and needles poking into him compresses my chest.

Jacob slips an arm around me. "It looks much worse than it is, sweetie. This morning the Doc here"—He gestures to Ledo—"told me they have to keep him sedated so he doesn't rip out his stitches."

Doc Ledo smiles reassuringly at us.

I stare at the friendly man who greeted us when we came in. Why is the veterinarian manning the front desk? No time to puzzle that out. I nod and smile.

"When can we take him home?" asks Jacob.

I can't make any words. I just stare at the bandages, and the images of that horrible night in the staircase replay, intercut with footage from that awful security tape.

"He'll have to stay at least until the weekend. We need to make sure there's no seepage."

At the word seepage, my full attention returns to the doctor. *Johnny Mnemonic*, starring Keanu Reeves, is one of my favorite movies of all time. Not a terribly popular choice with painfully poignant film-school students, but I like it. Seepage is one of the worst things that can happen in the movie. I cannot allow Pye to suffer any seepage.

"Can I stay with him?"

The doctor looks at me like I'm a little simple. "You want to stay here? At an animal hospital?"

For some reason the question offends me in my time of grief. I've seen women carry dogs in their purses. I can't be the first person who wanted to stay close to their beloved pet. "Yes. I'd like to stay in this room." I remember that I'm rich. "I'll have a cot brought in."

Jacob chuckles. "Sweetie, this isn't *Keeping up with the—*"

"I'm not leaving Pyewacket." I'm suddenly keenly aware of my attachment to this tan fur ball.

Doc Ledo nods politely. "I'm sure we can arrange something, Mitzy."

"I'm sure you can."

Ledo leaves without another word.

Jacob puts an arm around my shoulders. "Is the money going straight to your head?" He stifles a laugh.

"It might be," I admit as I blush.

He ruffles my hair as though I'm a six-year-old kid. "I don't deserve you."

I desperately attempt to repair my hairdo, be-fore I remember how I rolled out of bed and went directly to breakfast. I must've looked like warmed-over death when Erick saw me. Oh brother!

"I need to follow up with Cal's lawyer. Is it all right if I leave you here?"

"How will you get back? We drove quite a ways to get here." I touch my dad's arm in concern.

He pats my hand. "It's only a couple blocks back to Main Street. I took the long way here."

"I knew it!" I punch him playfully on the arm.

He hugs me. "Can I escort you to the Pin Cherry Festival tonight?"

"Absolutely not." I shake my head and cross my arms. "I'm sitting right here next to Pye until he's released."

Jacob shrugs. "Your loss. Tonight's the pin cherry pie-eating contest. I won three years in a row —back in the day."

"Tragic." I roll my eyes.

He laughs and leaves me in the sterile little room with nothing but the beep of machines to break the silence.

I scratch Pye's head right between his ears. "You are the most irritating mammal in the universe, Pyewacket. And I think I love you."

I swear he purrs.

CHAPTER 30

I SPEND THREE days doting on my four-legged savior. Odell brings me sustenance, and Silas takes messages to Grams.

By Friday evening my dad has had his fill. "I know I'm twenty-one years too late, Mitzy, but I'm pulling the dad card. I'm escorting you to the closing ceremonies of the Pin Cherry Festival tonight and I won't take 'no' for an answer."

I open my mouth to protest.

He crosses his arms and pinches his nose. "And someone has to tell you the truth about how badly you need a shower."

I look down at my "Free Contradictions $1.oo" tee and scrunch up my own nose. The truth hurts.

I scratch between Pye's tufted ears, lean over to him, and whisper, "I'll be back tomorrow. Don't do anything stupid—anything else stupid—before I get back."

His left front paw moves.

He's probably swatting a chunk of skin off my ankle in his drug-induced dream. Little adorable demon. I can see exactly why Grams spoiled him rotten. Looks like old Pyewacket has gotten himself another convert—perhaps I should say slave.

I look up at my dad's stubbornly crossed arms and exhale loudly. "All right, I'll go. I'm sure Grams would love to get me into another one of her vintage dresses."

I check out with Doc Ledo and make sure someone will be in the office on Saturday to let me in. Once Pyewacket's welfare has been secured, Jacob and I drive back to the bookshop.

He gives me a quick hug. "I'll go get cleaned up and be back to pick you up around 6:30. Sound good?"

"What about dinner?" I haven't had anything since Odell's breakfast special was delivered to my bedside vigil.

"There's a large food court at the festival. I'm sure you'll find a variety of fried things to devour."

"Rude." I grin and shake my head. I like food. What can I say? One day when my metabolism slows down . . . I'll worry about that later.

Once I'm safely over the chain and ensconced

in the dream closet, Grams fusses over dress selection.

"No. Red is too on the nose." She swirls down
the row again.

"You said that a half hour ago." I sink onto the
antique bench in the middle of the small room. "I'm
going to shower while you debate with yourself."

She barely acknowledges my exit. "Whatever
you say, dear."

I have to wash my hair twice. Truth time, the
shower was way overdue.

Back at closet headquarters, Grams has nar-
rowed the selection down to five semi-finalists. I immediately rule out three of the options as too
"foofy" for my current mood. I agree to try on the
remaining two finalists.

I don't hate the flowy white dress, but I plan to
eat at this festival. In the end, Grams and I agree on
the black, cherry-sequined dress by Altuzarra. It
definitely hits the theme on the head, and the dark
background ensures that any drops of pin cherry
will be camouflaged.

I attempt to recreate the sleek sophistication of
my ladies' luncheon hairdo.

"It's a good effort, honey."

Ghosts! Who knew they were so opinionated.

I grab a pair of black chunky heels with a delicate ankle strap. I need a solid heel to walk around

the festival grounds, but the single strap looks great with the embellished ruffle on the dress.

The intercom buzzes.

"Yes?"

My dad's voice comes through the speaker. "Ready?"

"Be right down."

I turn to Grams. "How do I look?"

"Gorgeous, smart. Maybe the sheriff will be there." She chuckles.

"Ha ha. I'm sure a lawman has better things to do than traipse around a fruit festival."

Grams nods fervently. "I'm sure you're right."

Her tone concerns me. I shake it off and hurry across the mezzanine.

As I circle down the staircase my dad lets out a low whistle. "Watch out, Pin Cherry! Mitzy Moon has arrived."

I blush. "Cut it out. You're my dad. You're supposed to be impressed."

He shakes his head. "If you don't spend most of the night dancing, I'll eat a pin cherry pie."

I laugh and hook my arm through his elbow. "That's not much of a compliment since I happen to know you can easily eat a pile of pies if there's a trophy at stake."

We take Dad's 1955 Ford F100 pickup. I take note that he drives his own vehicle at a calm, rational speed. I'm grateful to arrive at the fairgrounds without incident and breathing normally.

Even a big city girl like me has to admit that the festival looks magical. Edison lights hang in front of every booth as far as the eye can see, and the requisite cherry lights adorn hundreds of birch and pine along the border of the grounds.

A riff on "the gazebo" stands in the center of the fair. The six-sided structure is constructed from logs and resembles an old log cabin without walls.

A large, well-lit dance area wraps around the rotunda. I hope my dad is wrong about the dancing. Very wrong.

We make our way through the booths.

"Thanks for talking me into this, Dad. It's pretty fun."

His eyes widen in mock horror. "Just 'pretty fun?' I was thinking this could be my 'not a murderer' celebration. Seems like that should at least get a 'rad,' or whatever you kids are saying these days." The laughter lifts my spirits.

His mood is infectious and I hook my arm through his as I cheer, "Let's get turnt!"

He giggles like a schoolboy as he walks me toward a large pink-and-red canvas tent. "You have to try the deep-fried pin cherry ice cream," says Jacob.

I throw caution to the wind and give in to the dark side of cherry.

Cakes, cookies, relishes, sandwiches, smoothies, donuts . . . By the time I'm sipping my second red Solo Cup of pin cherry wine, I'm a dedicated fan of all things festive.

An older gentleman in a tuxedo with tails, and pin cherries adorning his top hat, steps up to the podium in the log-zebo.

"That's the mayor," whispers Jacob.

"Ladies and gentlemen, honored guests and dedicated residents, I'd like to invite Sheriff Harper to join me at the microphone.

Erick makes his way through the crowd, shaking hands and patting backs like a politician. As he climbs the steps, I nod. "Now there's a dessert I'd like to try."

Dad nudges me. "Mitzy, shhh."

All the color would drain from my face if my cheeks weren't artificially rosy from pin cherry wine. I honestly did not mean to say that out loud. I take a big sip of my wine and promise myself I'll blend in for the rest of the party.

While the sheriff explains the hallmarks of a Pin Cherry Festival Princess my attention wanders. Tilly and Tally stand across from me on the edge of the dance area.

They are cheering and clapping.

I catch their eye and wave.

They respond with frantically over-zealous waves. Then Tally points to the log-zebo.

It looks like she's gesturing for me to go up there. Does she know about my crush on the sheriff?

Jacob nudges me. "I'd get up there if I was you. It's worse if the Pin Cherry Patrol carries you on their shoulders."

Why is he laughing? And then I hear my name.

"Come on, Miss Moon." The sheriff waves me up to the stage. "Let's all give another round of applause to encourage our new Pin Cherry Festival Princess up to the mic."

Now the color truly does drain. Wine or no wine.

My own father gives me a firm push.

The crowd parts.

All sound vanishes from my world. The terror of this moment has me trapped in a slow-motion walk of shame.

Suddenly a cackle of delight breaks through.

The one and only Twiggy hoots and howls from her prime location right next to the steps.

I guess that answers the question of how my name got tossed into the hat for Pin Cherry Princess. Oh, my vengeance will be merciless.

The Pin Cherry Patrol swoops in and, before I can protect what's left of my dignity, I'm hoisted up on the shoulders of four burly high school boys and trucked up to the podium.

After they dump me unceremoniously on the dais, I stumble forward and suffer further embarrassment as Sheriff Erick grabs me around the waist to keep me from falling. Let the record show that he hesitates in removing his arm until well after I'm stabilized.

"Congratulations to Pin Cherry Harbor's newest resident and our new Princess!" The mayor slips a sash over my head to the thunderous cheers of the festivalgoers.

My face must be as red as a cherry.

"And now for the traditional dance. Take her for a spin, Sheriff." The mayor plops my hand into Erick's and shoves us toward the empty dance area.

I pinch myself mercilessly. If I can just wake up . . .

The sheriff leads me down the steps and spins me.

The shock of his dance skill snaps me out of wishing this was all a daydream. I count it a small mercy that I don't land on my backside.

Erick catches my hand in the nick of time and swirls me back into a "leave room for the holy spirit" respectable partners hold. "From murderer to princess in less than two weeks. What does the future hold for the indomitable Miss Moon?" His smile intrigues.

Time to get ahold of this thing. "I guess you'll have to stay tuned, Erick."

He grins and dips me.

The crowd goes wild. And a bunch of couples join in the dancing.

I nearly lose my sash.

He whips me upright and I can't help but notice the tiny beads of sweat on his brow. Oh, he plays the confident man about town, but it would seem that ol' Mitzy Moon still keeps him off balance.

The humble brag has no sooner formed in my mind than Erick catches that darn boot of his and we tumble onto the grass at the edge of the dance arena.

Once again, his Too Hot To Handle body breaks my fall.

Many hands scoop down and help us to our feet.

Lucky for me, Jacob is the first to grab my hand. He scoops an arm around me and shields me with his body. "Well, that was unfortunate." He chuckles.

"I'll say." I brush grass off my dress and smooth my hair. "I was just about to get the upper hand."

My dad laughs. "Come on, slugger. I'll get you a pin cherry brownie to make it all better."

I do not resist.

Silas stands next to the brownie booth and waves as we approach. "Ah, serendipity."

I shrug.

"I have news." He takes an unnecessarily large bite of his brownie.

Jacob gets two more, and the three of us head toward a park bench while Silas continues to chew.

He lifts the chocolate-cherry confection for another mouthful and I put up my hand. "Can we get the news?"

With regret in his eyes, he gently places the bar back on his napkin. "Kitty and Finnegan were arrested today."

I look at Jacob and raise my eyebrows.

He shakes his head.

"Don't keep us in suspense, Silas."

"Of course. Your tip about the fabricated charity led to an entire laundry list of charges. Not the least of which is her affair with Finnegan, which violates the fidelity clause in the pre-nuptial agreement she signed."

"Wait, I thought she said Finnegan was blackmailing her?"

Silas sneaks a small bite of his brownie and nods. "Oh, he was. He was entertaining the affair, commemorated it with photographs, and then blackmailed her when he found out about the pre-nup."

I chuckle. "No honor among thieves, I guess."

"Not that there ever was," my dad mumbles.

"Sorry, Dad."

"No worries. Not your fault." He shoves the rest of his treat into his mouth.

"I'm glad they won't be fleecing the town with another one of their fake Halloween balls." I clap my hands.

"Or inheriting," Silas adds.

My dad stops chewing. "Hmm?"

"Well, that trollop violated the pre-nup. In addition, Cal's attorney is in possession of the hand-written request for the alterations to the existing will, which she feels certain she can have declared valid as a holographic will."

I shake my head in confusion. "If it's a holograph, that means it doesn't actually exist, right?"

Silas shakes his head and his jowls wiggle in a way that my pin-cherry-wine-soaked brain finds hilarious.

He ignores my giggles. "Not with a will, Mitzy. A holographic will is a document written in the testator's own hand that serves as a legal last will and testament." He looks at my face and adds, "The testator in this case is Cal."

I smile and nod.

Jacob wipes the chocolate from the corner of his mouth and stares at Silas. "What does that mean?"

"Since Kitty is in no position to contest the holographic will, it means that you are Cal's rightful heir. As he intended."

Jacob chews the inside of his cheek and puts an arm around my shoulders. "And my daughter?"

"Mitzy will be the contingent beneficiary; again, per Cal's wishes."

I reach up and squeeze my dad's hand. "Does this mean you'll stay in town?"

"I don't know, Mitzy. I'd have to quit my job."

"Oh, sorry. I didn't realize—"

"You didn't let me finish. I'd have to quit my job delivering pizzas."

I look from him to Silas and back.

"Ex-con joke. Probably not the right crowd." He gives me a little hug. "I'll move to Pin Cherry on one—make that two—conditions."

"Which are?" I lean back and narrow my gaze.

"You promise to have breakfast with me every Sunday morning at Myrtle's Diner—"

"Done. What's the second?"

"You allow me the honor of purchasing all of Pyewacket's Fruity Puffs until he or I leave this earth."

Silas chuckles until his hound-dog cheeks turn red.

I hug my dad tightly, but selfishly find myself wishing one of his conditions had included another dance for Sheriff Erick and me.

Squad goals. A girl's gotta have goals.

End of Book 1

But, the mysteries continue...
Curl up with the next book in the Mitzy Moon
Mysteries series!

A NOTE FROM TRIXIE

Wow! Ten months ago I was outlining this book and wondering if anyone would ever get to meet Mitzy. But here we are!

One of the best parts of bringing Mitzy to life was the wonderful feedback from my early readers. Thank you to my alpha readers Angel, Michael, and Andrew. HUGE thanks to my fantastic beta readers who gave me extremely useful and honest feedback: Veronica McIntyre, Renee Arthur, Nadine Peterse-Vrijhof, and Lori Watson. And big hugs to the world's best ARC Team – Trixie's Mystery ARC Detectives!

Thank you to my brilliant editor Philip Newey! Some authors dread edits, but it was a pleasure to work with Philip, and I look forward to many more. Any remaining errors are my own.

Google can give an author all kinds of helpful information, but there is absolutely no substitute for "straight from the horse's mouth." Thanks to my "horses!" John Girard, thank you for answering my inane questions about what it was like to be a correctional officer. Your insights gave the character of Jacob a great deal more authenticity. Morgan, thank you for giving me the straight talk I needed to add some edge to Odell's Army backstory and, of course, your firearms expertise will never go to waste. And finally, thank you to Josh for all the years you begged for a caracal! I was never as brave as Grams, but your passion for them sent me down the "rabbit hole" and once I learned all I could about the little beasts—I knew I had to have one—even if it lives only in my mind.

Now I'm writing book four in the Mitzy Moon Mysteries series, and I think I may just live in Pin Cherry Harbor forever. Mitzy, Grams, and Pyewacket continue to get into trouble in book two, *Tattoos and Clues*. But I'd have to say that book three, *Wings and Broken Things*, is when most readers say the series becomes unputdownable.

I hope you'll continue to hang out with us.

Trixie Silvertale (October 2019)

Mitzy Moon Mysteries #2

A beachside stroll. A deadly discovery. Will this psychic sleuth swim or sink?

Mitzy wishes she could turn a blind third-eye to her hit-or-miss powers. Instead, while taking her fiendish feline for a walk, they make a stomach-churning find on shore. Despite her loss of appetite, she can't help but get a closer look at the unique ink etched into the corpse...

Before she can track down the killer, Mitzy must sweet-talk her way off the sexy sheriff's suspect list. And once again her meddling Ghost-ma is dying to interfere with the case. But when the trail leads to dangerous smugglers who shoot first and don't ask questions, she could end up in over her head...

Can Mitzy uncover the truth, or will hers be the next body to float to the surface?

Tattoos and Clues is the second book in the hilarious paranormal cozy mystery series, Mitzy Moon Mysteries. If you like snarky heroines, supernatural intrigue, and a dash of romance, then you'll love Trixie Silvertale's twisty whodunits.

Buy *Tattoos and Clues* to unravel a black market mystery today!

Grab yours here!
readerlinks.com/l/5211996

Scan this QR Code with the camera on your phone. You'll be taken right to the next case!

SPECIAL INVITATION . . .

Come visit Pin Cherry Harbor!

Get access to the Exclusive Mitzy Moon Mysteries character quiz – free!

Find out which character you are in Pin Cherry Harbor and see if you have what it takes to be part of Mitzy's gang.

This quiz is only available to members of the Paranormal Cozy Club, Trixie Silvertale's Facebook readers group.

Visit the link below to join the club and get access to the quiz:

Join Trixie's Club

https://trixiesilvertale.com/paranormal-cozy-club/

Once you're in the Club, you'll also be the first to receive updates from Pin Cherry Harbor and access to giveaways, new release announcements, behind-the-scenes secrets, and much more!

Scan this QR Code with the camera on your phone. You'll be taken right to the page to join the Club!

THANK YOU!

Trying out a new book is always a risk and I'm thankful that you rolled the dice with Mitzy Moon. If you loved the book, the sweetest thing you can do (*even sweeter than pin cherry pie à la mode*) is to leave a review so that other readers will take a chance on Mitzy and the gang.

Don't feel you have to write a book report. A brief comment like, "Can't wait to read the next book in this series!" will help potential readers make their choice.

★★★★★

Leave a quick review HERE

https://readerlinks.com/l/791849

Thank you kindly, and I'll see you in Pin Cherry Harbor!

ALSO BY TRIXIE SILVERTALE

Mitzy Moon Mysteries
Paranormal Cozy Mysteries

Fries and Alibis

Tattoos and Clues

Wings and Broken Things

Sparks and Landmarks

Charms and Firearms

Bars and Boxcars

Swords and Fallen Lords

Wakes and High Stakes

Tracks and Flashbacks

Lies and Pumpkin Pies

Hopes and Slippery Slopes

Hearts and Dark Arts

Dames and Deadly Games

Castaways and Longer Days

Schemes and Bad Dreams

Carols and Yule Perils

Dangers and Empty Mangers

Heists and Poltergeists

Blades and Bridesmaids

Scones and Tombstones

Vandals and Yule Scandals

Harper and Moon Investigations
Paranormal Cozy Mysteries

Ropes and Last Hopes

Bells and Bombshells

Rodeo Clowns and Shakedowns

Stiffs and Petroglyphs

Fatal Wines and Valentines

April Curses and May Hearses

Wheels and Dirty Deals

Scripts and Empty Crypts

Christmas Catastrophe Mysteries
Culinary Cozy Mysteries

Peppermint Cookie Murder

Apple Dumpling Murder

Linzer Cookie Murder

Chocolate Crinkle Cookie Murder

...more to come!

MAGICAL RENAISSANCE FAIRE MYSTERIES

Explore the world of Coriander the Conjurer. A fortune-telling fairy with a heart of gold!

Book 1:

All Swell That Ends Spell – A dubious festival. A fatal swim. Can this fortune-telling fairy herald the true killer?

Book 2:

Fairy Wives of Windsor – A jolly Faire. A shocking murder. Can this furtive fairy outsmart the killer?

Book 3:

Double Double Royal Trouble – When a treat-peddling witch is found dead, will this cursed faire crumble?

Join Sydney Coleman and her unruly ghosts, as they solve mysteries in a truly haunted mansion!

Book 1: **Moonlight and Mischief** – She's desperate for a fresh start, but is a mansion on sale too good to be true?

Book 2: **Moonlight and Magic** – A haunted Halloween tour seem like the perfect plan, until there's murder...

Book 3: ***Moonlight and Mayhem*** – An unwelcome visitor. A surprising past. Will her fire sale end in smoke?

ABOUT THE AUTHOR

USA TODAY Bestselling author Trixie Silvertale grew up reading an endless supply of Lilian Jackson Braun, Hardy Boys, and Nancy Drew novels. She loves the amateur sleuths in cozy mysteries and obsesses about all things paranormal. Those two passions unite in all her cozy mysteries, and she's thrilled to write them and share them with you.

When she's not consumed by writing, she bakes to fuel her creative engine and pulls weeds in her herb garden to clear her head (*and sometimes she pulls out her hair, but mostly weeds*).

Greetings are welcome:
trixie@trixiesilvertale.com

f facebook.com/TrixieSilvertale

◎ instagram.com/trixiesilvertale

BB bookbub.com/authors/trixie-silvertale